WHEN THE
FOG CLEARED

BEKAH FERGUSON

This book is a work of fiction. Names, characters, places and incidents are either the product of the author's imagination or are used fictitiously. Any resemblance to actual events or locales or persons, living or dead, is entirely coincidental.

This book is published by:
Rock of Ages Publishing House
A Division of Prodigy Digital Solutions
5-190 Minet's Point Road, Suite 251
Barrie, Ontario Canada L4N 8J8

Printed in the United States of America

ALSO AVAILABLE ON KINDLE

ISBN-13: 978-0-9782047-7-8

10 9 8 7 6 5 4 3 2

For my beta readers,
Hillary Handy, Rachel Xu,
Abby Page, and Robbie Ferguson.
As a team you helped me bring
this novel to the next level,
and I am deeply grateful.

She relived a starry night when she and Drew had walked that same shoreline arm in arm. Both barefoot, tingling water engulfing their ankles before releasing to slide back across the sand. She wore a summer halter dress, grey cast in the moon-light, and he khaki shorts with a tee. His black hair, tousled, glimmered, just like his eyes when he smiled. His arm was warm, his whole side warm, and she leaned into him, nestling her cheek against his shoulder. They watched whitecaps dance across the distant waters. He stroked her hair and kissed her cheekbone, so tender. Her heart was full. Later they went inside . . . opened the bedroom windows to let in the melody of the waves . . . and made love under soft lamplight.

Gone.

All gone now.

CHAPTER 1

The Isle of Devils may seem a curious travel desti-
nation for a woman escaping her demons. But
Kylie Cadore's ship was sinking back in Canada,
not these treacherous seas.

The taxi cab pulled to a stop at the entrance
gates of an estate, and Kylie stepped out, stretching
her arms. Her two little girls clambered out as well,
going straight to the closed gate ahead. There they
fidgeted, touching the iron poles and kicking peb-
bles as Kylie rang the house on the keypad. Several
attempts brought no answer so she punched in the
passcode herself. The well-oiled gates opened and
they entered the property, the girls running ahead
like a pair of sprites.

A Hawthorne-yellow Georgian home stood
far ahead, built on a Bermudian hill overlooking

the sea.

Her father's house.

Poinciana trees lined both sides of the driveway in scarlet-flowered blossom. A breeze tossed petals across her feet as she walked, the scent of rain in the air. Beyond the estate whitecaps tripped across the distant waters, palm fronds stretching with a gust of wind.

They reached the house and the children climbed the steps of the front portico, laughing. Kylie lifted her chin, breathing in for strength.

Memories of Drew were everywhere.

The shade beneath the palmetto where they first kissed. The moongate leading into the garden where he proposed.

Quickening her pace, she forced her thoughts to the present and tugged a suitcase up the steps, hoping her father would be pleased to see them. Her decision to come here for the month of July was impromptu; she hadn't confirmed an arrival date with him, though he knew she planned to visit during the summer. Originally she'd intended to wait for August but last minute had decided to come right away once school was out; feeling restless and impatient, and needing a change of scenery. She'd gotten a deal on tickets too and figured she'd surprise him by just showing up. It was likely no one was home right now, since no answer had come at the gate, but she assumed at least the housekeeper was there and would let them in.

"Okay, girls," she said, smoothing their wind-tousled hair, "ready to see Grandpa?"

They nodded eagerly. Kylie rang the bell and they waited.

After no immediate answer, she rang again, and when a full minute had passed, tried the knob.

The door swung open.

Odd.

Or was it? If her father's girlfriend was home, maybe she didn't feel the need to keep the house locked.

With a shrug, Kylie dragged her luggage inside and motioned for the girls to follow.

Rooms fanned out on either side of the hallway, and to the right, a cedar staircase twirled to the second floor. The wistful guitar strains and yearning vibrato of Portuguese Fado music filtered down the hallway.

Someone must be home after all.

"Hello?" she called out with a cheerful lilt. "Hello?" This time louder.

"Stay here, girls, I'll be right back." Mya and Keira plunked down on the bottom step of the staircase and Kylie followed the music to the back of the house.

"Hello? Anyone home?"

Her father's housekeeper poked her head out of the open doors to the library, eyes widening. "Mrs. Cadore—but when did you get here?"

Kylie grinned with relief. "Connie! We just arrived. Where is everybody?"

The housekeeper stepped out into the hallway, cheeks mottled. She glanced back over her shoulder.

"Is something the matter?"

Connie moved around Kylie without a word and motioned for her to follow. They dipped into the music room and the middle-aged woman, her hair white and pixie cut, leaned against the grand piano. She spoke in a hushed tone. "Did Mr. Patterson—I mean, your father—did he know about your coming today?"

Kylie shook her head. "No, I thought I'd surprise him this time." She smiled, stomach tightening; something had to be wrong. "Is he away?"

Connie glanced toward the open doorway and dropped her voice to a whisper. "It's rather unfortunate you didn't call ahead and let us know exactly when you'd be coming," she said. "It's really not a good day for you to be here. We're just waiting for," —she knit her brow— "well, it's not the greatest timing, Mrs. Cadore. Your father's in St. George and will be back tomorrow. It's . . . Pearl. She's . . . " A puff of air escaped her lips. "Well, she's having a bad day."

Kylie stared at the housekeeper. "What do you mean 'a bad day'?"

Her lips parted but she didn't speak.

"Connie?"

"She's . . . she's fine . . . it's just that she doesn't want to be seen by anyone right now."

"Is she sick?"

Connie maintained eye contact but didn't respond. Kylie turned and went to the doorway; she would find Pearl and see for herself.

"You mustn't go to her. She wants privacy."

Kylie hesitated. Pearl was her father's common-law wife—surely she wouldn't mind her would-be step-daughter knowing she was ill.

"Are the children with you?" Connie asked.

"Yes, of course. They're at the front door."

"Come with me to the kitchen then. I'll whip up a nice little snack for everyone. It's nearly tea time, I'll throw on the kettle."

"I need to know what's the matter first." Kylie headed for the hallway. "Please though," she said over her shoulder, "do take Mya and Keira to the kitchen with you, I'd really appreciate that. They'll be hungry for sure."

Connie looked distressed but gave a nod of consent and made her way to the front entrance. Kylie went to the library across the hall, palms clammy at her sides.

The mournful guitar music continued to filter from the room. She paused on the threshold, then went inside.

In a brocade wing chair positioned toward the fireplace sat her father's rather young girlfriend, Pearl Airoso; only ten years older than Kylie. She was hunched forward wearing a dressing gown and trembling all over, wet hair dangling about her face.

Kylie took a tentative step forward.

"Ramiro, is that you?" the voice cracked part way through as though she'd been crying, or perhaps coughing. She didn't look up.

Kylie hurried forward across the hardwood, maneuvering around a brown leather sofa and rounding the chair.

She reached for the woman's shoulder but Pearl recoiled at the touch, eyes widening with a look of shock.

"Pearl, what's wrong?"

"N-nothing. I am fine, I am fine. Please go away." She pulled herself to a standing position, still shaking, and moved from the chair, hair obscuring her face again. Kylie stepped completely out of the way. "Leave me," Pearl cried out, raising her voice. "I do not want to be seen like this." She stumbled into an end table next to one of the sofas, knocking a porcelain vase and its contents to the floor. It shattered across the hardwood in a puddle of water and blue-eyed grass flowers.

Kylie headed for the door, heart drumming in her chest. "I'm calling Dad," she said over her shoulder.

A feral sound escaped the woman's lips and she lunged toward Kylie, stopping short at a coffee table in her way. She struggled to balance herself. "Do not do it, please, do not."

Kylie took another step toward the door.

"Please, I can not have him see me like this, I could not bare it. I already have help coming—he will be here any minute—please believe me."

He?

"Tell me what's wrong then." This she said with a gentle tone.

Pearl sunk down on the sofa. The tremors were ceasing and a stillness came over her body. She pushed her hair up off her face. "Please," she said through bloodless lips, "it is not an emergency, you must believe me. It is not as bad as it looks." Her droopy eyes flashed open, full and chestnut. "I am fine now."

"But you're white as a ghost."

"Please do not call your father," Pearl repeated, gaze boring into Kylie's as though attempting to cast a spell. "This is none of your business," she said, "and you do not have the right to interfere. Do you understand that?" Her voice more desperate than condescending.

Kylie fisted her hands and turned on her heel.

Emerging into the hallway, she collided with a handsome, well-dressed man who'd apparently been about to enter the library.

"My dear, I'm so sorry," he said with surprise, catching her in his arms and looking down at her. He held her at arm's length a moment and let go, a half-grin playing on his lips.

In one glance she took in his striking features—the tanned skin, well-cut nose, mocha irises.

"I'm sorry," she sputtered. "Who are you? Have we met before?"

CHAPTER 2

A honeyed smile spread across the man's lips. "No, my dear, I don't think I've ever had the pleasure." A hybrid accent laced his words and he looked to be mid-thirties. "You're Edward's daughter, yes? I recognize you from the photos on the mantel." He stuck out his hand and she took it. "I am Ramiro Airoso. Pearl's cousin."

"Oh!" She glanced back into the library. "Are you here to help?"

A grave nod. "Yes." He smiled then. "But it's absolutely nothing to worry about, I assure you. She'll be quite fine. There is no need to contact Mr. Patterson. In fact, may I have your word that you will not?"

She wondered if he'd been listening for a while from the hallway, out of sight. "I won't call him just now," she said with an exhale, "so long as Pearl can show me that she's really okay."

"Excellent, thank you. Now, if you'll excuse me?" He lifted a perfect eyebrow and she nodded, moving aside so he could enter the room.

Leaving him to it, she went to collect her luggage; which still sat at the entrance unattended. Her initial intention had been to phone and ask her father what was going on but it was clear now that he didn't know and was also being deceived in some manner. She needed to quiz Connie later and see what she could find out.

Glancing up at the tall window above the door, she hefted the backpack over one shoulder and took hold of the suitcase handle. The rain had yet to come. She might as well put the luggage away first before seeking out her children; they were no doubt sitting happily with some goodie in the kitchen while Connie fussed over them.

She pulled the suitcase up the stairs and wheeled it to the far end of the second floor where the guest rooms were located. Her father had decorated one of the rooms specifically for his only two grandchildren, with honeydew walls and canopied twin beds. She went inside and set the suitcase on one of the pink coverlets next to a pile of teddy bears and baby dolls, unpacking it. She then wheeled the rest of the luggage to the bedroom down the hall. Two windows in the corner room looked out over the sloping yard and coastline from one wall, and the garden and cedar grove from another. The ocean could be seen for miles. The windows were open, a salty breeze swaying the curtains from time to time.

She placed her clothes in an empty dresser facing the foot of the bed, noticing a white and blue box of Band-Aids in the back corner of the bottom drawer. A previous guest must have forgotten it there. With a shrug, she let it be and finished unpacking. In the ensuite bathroom, she tidied her ringlet curls to freshen her appearance, and felt satisfied when the dark swirls settled about her chin and the nape of her neck.

She glanced at her wristwatch. It was nearly four o'clock; teatime. As a British colony, Bermuda practised the same afternoon teatime tradition as Britain. Although, with Pearl's health issue, perhaps Connie would forgo the daily custom today. Nevertheless, she'd better find out. Changing out of her travelling clothes into a white eyelet dress and pink cardigan, she went downstairs in search of her children.

The front door whooshed open as she reached the bottom of the staircase—her brother stepping inside with a forceful gust of wind. He pushed the door shut and turned around, giving her a startled look and relaxing only slightly when he realized who she was.

"Kylie—!" A flicker of eye contact but no smile. "What are you doing here?"

"Hello to you, too, Trey," she grinned, moving off the last stair and giving him a hug. He stood as still as a post, enduring the embrace as though it came from a stranger on the street. Granted, she hadn't seen him in person in nearly two years.

"Are you coming to tea?" she asked.

He glanced down the hall, then met her eyes through the curls obscuring his own. "No. Don't usually. I've got some stuff going on." Though he was twenty-three, his chest and shoulders were narrow, giving him the in-between look of a boy who is not quite a man.

Without warning he moved around her and began mounting the stairs, mumbling over his shoulder that he'd see her around.

With a shrug, she made her way down the hall to the library, half-expecting to find Pearl still sitting on the wing chair in her dressing gown. Instead, she found her daughters perched side-by-side on a sofa; Keira's little legs too short to reach the floor. Connie was bent over a table pouring tea into China cups. The broken pottery and flowers were all cleaned up and gone.

Kylie helped herself to a plate of cucumber sandwich squares and indulged in one shortbread cookie as well, taking a seat next to the children. Fado music continued to play from a stereo nestled in the bookshelves.

"Have the girls eaten?" she asked, taking the proffered teacup from Connie. The housekeeper nodded. "Yes, ma'am. Though I'm afraid I may've spoiled their suppers." Kylie laughed and they chatted casually for a few minutes until footsteps sounded in the hall and Pearl entered the room with her cousin, Ramiro.

She had changed into a yellow dress; a feather necklace dangling over her slight cleavage. Coffee-brown hair hung in flowing waves and her previously pale lips were full and red. They spread into a sweet, genuine smile for the children as she said hello. After introducing Ramiro to the girls, she took a teacup from Connie, sat down on an adjacent sofa, and crossed her overly toned legs on a severe slant as though posing for a fashion magazine.

Kylie looked away to avoid rolling her eyes. Ramiro sat down next to Pearl and smiled a silent greeting. She met his gaze, a warm tingle moving through her, and she took a sip of tea to distract herself.

The girls were growing antsy, so she dismissed them with the suggestion that they go upstairs and play with the toys in the bedroom.

"How have you been, Kylie?" Pearl began with a hybrid accent of Portuguese and British influence, strikingly similar to Ramiro's. She sipped her tea with ease and composure, smiling intermittently at her cousin. It was as though nothing had happened at all; as though Kylie had only just now arrived and this was their first encounter.

"I've been well, thank you." It was far from the truth.

An image of Drew filled her mind but she blinked it away.

"Dad's been expecting me to visit this summer," she said, "as you probably know. So, I thought I'd surprise him. But I'm really sorry for intruding earlier, I should have called ahead from the airport." She sensed Ramiro studying her, though she didn't turn to face him. Instead, she smoothed the folds of her skirt over her knees and accepted a refill of tea from Connie, who hovered about them.

"Yes, calling ahead would have been a good idea . . . so that we might have been prepared, of course." There was a touch of coldness in her voice but a kind smile on her lips. "At any rate," she went on in a pleasant tone, "your father will be quite thrilled to see you, he likes surprises. He often laments how infrequently he gets to see you and the children." The smile strained a little then. "He will be home tomorrow. I will keep your secret for you so that when he arrives, it will still be a surprise. How long will you be staying?"

"If it's alright with Dad, and you . . . I'd like to stay till the end of July?"

With the children out of school and needing to be entertained, a month in Bermuda seemed like the perfect way to pass half the summer.

Pearl gave a slow nod in response but looked uncertain, gazing at Kylie over a finely cut nose. If she felt imposed upon she took pains to hide it. She lifted her cup from the saucer in her hand and took a sip. It clinked as she set it back down. "You will have to talk to Eddie—your father, rather—about your length of stay," she said, voice warbling on the last word.

It was Kylie's father in fact who had suggested she stay a whole month, back in the spring when they'd discussed a potential visit; and she'd assumed Pearl was fine with that. Maybe she wasn't.

Kylie glanced at Ramiro. He smiled and his eyes danced a little, as though sharing a private joke with her. She gave a slight smile in return, unsure how to respond.

"Kylie," Pearl continued.

"Mm?"

"Are you still teaching?"

"Oh yes." She was a music teacher at an elementary school in Ontario and took great satisfaction in watching young students foster an interest in music. The past several months had been a great strain however; having to put on a happy face when she felt nothing of the sort. As a classically trained violinist, she'd once played for the beauty and joy of the art, but now she played mostly as an outlet for the bitter emotions churning within.

"That is nice for you," Pearl said after a few seconds of thoughtful silence, rubbing the rim of her saucer with a manicured index finger. "Not everyone has the luxury of taking summers off from work."

A strange comment coming from someone who hadn't worked in over two years. Pearl had been an esthetician for a whole decade, resigning when a back injury made full-time work impossible. The injury had long since healed; as far as Kylie knew anyway.

Pearl seemed lost in her private thoughts again, a silence growing between them. Not a comfortable silence either. More of an edgy one, leaving Kylie ill at ease, fidgety, unsure of her place or welcome. They weren't close; seeing each other only once every couple of years made it difficult to get to know one another. And Pearl seldom participated when Kylie's father called on Skype.

Kylie turned to face Ramiro again, feeling obligated to make conversation with at least one of them, but he showed no signs of discomfort at all; evidently content to sit back and watch the two women without joining in himself.

"So, you said you and Pearl are cousins?"

"Indeed." A smooth smile, eyes warm and bright. Intelligent. "I stop in to visit whenever I'm on the Island."

She nodded, put on a smile of her own. "Where are you from?"

"Oh, I live here." He leaned back in the seat, stretched his legs out. They were nice legs, long and lean. "But I work on a cruise ship."

"Kylie," Pearl interrupted, "may I be candid with you?"

"Yes?"

"What . . . happened . . . this afternoon," — she seemed to be choosing her words carefully — "I am quite sorry that you had to see that." She pulled herself up a little. "It was not very becoming of me and I was embarrassed to be seen in such a manner, as I am sure you can appreciate." A pointed look. "I am very private about my health and therefore do not wish to worry your father." Something sparked in her eyes at that. Not anger though. Fear? "As I mentioned before," she continued, "your father is unaware of my, condition, and it is the way I wish for things to remain." A pause. "Can I trust you to keep this matter strictly between you and I?"

Kylie looked at Ramiro. "Is it true?" she asked. "That it isn't something serious? It looked serious."

He disarmed her with a smile. "Absolutely no worries, my dear, no worries at all." He folded his hands over his tight midsection. "Pearl is a strong and capable woman and if there were any true cause for concern, she would be the first to tell Edward herself. You can rest assured of that."

"Alright, Pearl," she acquiesced. "I won't mention this to Dad, but it does put me in an awkward position—you know I don't like keeping anything from him—and he'll hate to be kept in the dark if you have a medical condition."

Pearl blinked, then smiled. Stood. "Excuse me, I must go now." She passed her cup and saucer off to Connie, hands shaking slightly, and left the room, heels clicking on the hardwood.

Ramiro stood too and reached out to shake Kylie's hand with a warm, strong grip. She stared at him, shaken by Pearl's sudden departure.

"It's been a pleasure to have met you," he

said, looking unfazed, "but I must be taking my leave as well." He glanced at his watch. "I've a few things to do downtown, so, until next time."

Left alone, save for Connie, who was clearing away the tea things, Kylie went to a window and moved aside the drape.

She stood staring out over the backyard for some time, though specks of water on the window pane marred the view. Rain had begun and palm fronds leaned in the wind, the sea frothing in the distance.

Eventually she looked down at her hands, splaying her fingers.

Her ring finger was pale where her wedding band had covered it for ten years. In time the ring of white would tan enough to match her normal skin tone, but for now it stood out as a beacon.

To both her and anyone else who might have interest in examining her hand for personal details.

CHAPTER 3

Andrew Cadore left the golf club where he worked as an instructor, and stepped out into the heat; donning his sunglasses as he walked across the baked parking lot. He climbed into his oven-like sedan and checked his phone, hoping for a new text from Kylie. Nothing. She'd at least sent him a brief one earlier after arriving at the airport in Bermuda, to let him know they'd arrived safely. He sent a quick message asking her to call, then started the engine. A bead of sweat slid down his forehead, t-shirt damp and clinging to him. He rolled down the windows and leaned back against the headrest, shutting his eyes a moment.

He pictured her at the altar: a vision that had haunted him the past few weeks. But it wasn't the altar they'd once stood at together. The groom

—not him. Instead, some blurry-faced stud, tuxedoed shoulders back; Kylie gazing up into his eyes with that same brilliant smile she used to give Drew. And there, his two little girls, flower girls, coming up the aisle tossing rose petals.

Drew opened his eyes and drove the twenty minutes across the city to the bachelor apartment he rented in his brother's basement. To keep himself distracted, he listened to talk radio instead of music. Nothing but shadows met him inside the unadorned apartment and he switched on a light before tossing his keys on the kitchenette counter. They clinked as they made contact—sliding across the surface and hitting a pile of junk mail.

He checked his phone again. One missed call. From Kylie. Seriously, while he was driving? It figured. She was probably relieved not to have to talk to him too.

"I should have called sooner," the voicemail began, "but it's been a long day. We arrived at Dad's early afternoon. The kids are fine. Anyway, you're probably eating dinner right now, so I'll have the kids give you a call later this evening before they go to bed. Bye for now."

Drew stood fixed in place, feeling more isolated than ever. He hadn't been looking forward to this. Four and a half weeks without seeing his daughters. A whole month of being alone.

Of purgatory.

Yes, it was true he'd reluctantly agreed to let them go when Kylie asked him about the trip a few weeks ago, but only because he didn't want to be selfish. Mya and Keira would love the time with their grandfather, and it was summer after all.

Darkness pressed in on his heart and he felt the void: a pang in his chest as he breathed in and out, and a tightness between his shoulders. After months of stress, of living in limbo, he was emotionally exhausted.

She called again in the evening as promised but only spoke long enough to transfer the phone to their oldest daughter. Drew put on a cheery tone; eager to hear their little munchkin voices and already missing them. Keira came on the line after Mya but the phone disconnected before he could ask to speak to their mother again. No surprise there. He doubted he'd hear two words from her the entire time she was away.

With nothing else to do but not tired enough to go to sleep, he decided to put on a mindless action movie. The room grew darker by degrees as evening fell. When the film ended two hours later, he felt a familiar tug at the core of his being. His breathing shallowed. If he was a drinking man, the bottle would offer comfort, but he refused to buy it anymore—at least, as long as he remained in this particular state of depression. He and Kylie had separated only four months prior and an overwhelming urge for alcohol had seized him time and again in his darkest hours. Much like a ravenous appetite or a physical entity beckoning him. But he knew his weaknesses well enough by now to recognize the assured risk of addiction in his nature. Drinking for comfort would be disastrous. The one night he did buy a bottle of wine, he downed it entirely within one evening. That's when he knew what he was up against; and hadn't drank another glass since.

Besides, drunkenness was no less a vice than the one that wrecked his marriage in the first place.

Rising from the couch, he went to his bedroom and switched on a floor fan but not the light. He shucked off his clothes except his boxers, and climbed into the double bed.

The room was dark and stuffy. Light from a street lamp streamed through the window blinds casting a pattern of slats across the unadorned wall to his right. He let his eyes focus on the lines until his vision grew blurry; the lines merging together.

After a while he grew much too hot and

kicked off the blanket, rolling over, aware of the empty space next to him. He shut his eyes and lay perfectly still. The anxiety, the temptation—for what he must not and could not have—would torment him until he fell asleep.

Some thirsts were not meant to be quenched.

At least, not from the proffered cup.

What he really wanted was to be with Kylie, but Kylie was gone.

Kylie awakened at predawn to the low murmur of the sea.

Boney light from the moon suffused the contours of the bedroom furniture. She sat up and pushed aside her blankets, stepping out of the queen bed and into her slippers. With a yawn, she padded across the hardwood to one of the open windows overlooking the water. Down below was the sloping backyard that led to the beach beyond. Seagrapes and mangroves on each side of the cove-like beach resembled boulders in the dark; lanky palms rising above them here and there. The palms were unmoving, leaves hanging, the wind no longer blowing. The sea had calmed too, its waters dark as tar.

The beach sand glowed in contrast to its bleak surroundings, white instead of its usual pink.

She pulled up an armchair, sat down, and breathed in the scent of cedar and saltwater coming in through the screen. In a half-awake state she watched the seascape morph and change as the sun rose.

Later, after getting the children up and dressed, Kylie took them downstairs to the dining room for breakfast. Golden sunlight poured through the window panes, bouncing off the polished dining table and gilded picture frames. Connie had already set the table with silverware and linen napkins. A vase of calla lilies sat in the center; beside it, orange juice, maple syrup, and a dish of curled butter balls. The scent of sausages and brewing coffee wafted from the kitchen, drawing them to their seats.

They had only just seated themselves when Pearl entered the room wearing tennis garb, her hair swept up into a twist under a visor.

"Good morning everyone," she said, smiling a greeting at Kylie and the girls as she took her seat at the head of the table. Her brown eyes were bright and cheerful though evident concealer had been applied beneath, suggesting somewhat of an illusion.

Connie entered the room holding a plate piled with steaming pancakes in one hand and a dish of browned sausages in the other. On weekends meals were a free-for-all, but during the week Connie served breakfast, lunch, and tea time. Kylie offered to say a prayer of thanksgiving for the food, and everyone took turns helping themselves. Pearl took two pancakes and ate them plain. She drank her tea black as well. Kylie, noting this, wavered over the butter and sausages, mentally comparing her own calves to Pearl's: hers weren't nearly as sculpted in a pair of heels. She wondered if she ought to put more effort into losing five pounds by cutting back on calories. Then again, doing so might decrease her curves, which seemed counter-productive. Maybe she ought to work out for longer increments then, push harder. Though Pearl was ten years her senior, she was lean and sinewy, having the chiseled, hard-looking body of an athlete. Kylie felt almost frumpy in comparison; she was slender, but soft rather than defined.

With an inaudible sigh, Kylie passed on the butter but not the syrup. She took two sausages instead of three and decided to forgo sugar in her coffee, even though she disliked the bitter taste. Though she wished to be tightly toned like Pearl, she could never put in the two hours a day of exercising it required—as her father once mentioned was his girlfriend's regimen.

Trey entered the room as Kylie took her first bite of pancake. With a nod and flicker of eye contact, he took a seat next to her and filled his plate, sloshing a pool of syrup over it all. The children eyed him curiously but said little.

Pearl ignored his presence altogether, barely glancing his way when he first sat down. She was focused on her pancakes, cutting slices one at a time, and lifting each bite to her red lips in a methodical way. Each bite was chewed slowly and thoughtfully, perhaps pureed to oblivion before swallowed.

Kylie took a sip of coffee and tried not to cringe. It wasn't too late to add sugar but she couldn't bring herself to do it with Pearl sitting right there.

The front doorbell chimed and Pearl excused herself.

"So, how have you been, Trey?" Kylie asked, looking at her brother and hoping he would talk now that Pearl wasn't in the room. He hadn't joined them for supper the night before; a simple affair, with Kylie and Pearl straining to make small talk in the absence of Edward.

Trey gave her a quick look through his curls. "I'm fine, nothing new," he said, stuffing a final forkful of pancake in his mouth. He'd devoured his breakfast already. Declining the tea

Connie was offering to pour him, he began to fidget.

"Can we go swimming today?" Mya asked before Kylie could figure out what to say to her brother next.

She grinned. "Why sure—that's what we're here for, silly! After lunch would be a good time because this morning I thought we might ride into town and do a little window shopping. What do you think?"

Mya considered this and nodded, her long black hair bobbing up and down. She rhymed off several items she wanted but Keira paid no mind to the conversation. She was too busy attempting to spear a sausage, both hands wrapped around the fork as she aimed.

Kylie laughed and took another sip of coffee. Not holding back the cringe this time, she reached for the bowl of sugar as footsteps sounded in the hall.

She turned in her seat as Pearl entered the room, followed by Ramiro Airoso. He too was dressed in tennis garb, a racket in hand.

She ditched the sugar.

CHAPTER 4

"Good-morning everyone," Ramiro said, his smile lingering on Kylie. Her stomach did a flip-flop.

Trey dropped out of his chair, brushed past Ramiro with his head down and went out the door.

"Everyone—we must be going," Pearl said, rising. "I am sorry to have to leave you so abruptly. Do be sure to let Connie know if you will be here for lunch. I will not be, as I intend to run some errands after tennis."

Ramiro bid them good-day and followed Pearl from the room, leaving Kylie with the sensation of sunlight disappearing behind clouds.

An hour later, she and the children were seated side-by-side on a pink transit bus, headed for downtown Hamilton.

After a time of winding along the narrow bedrock roads, flanked by palms, cedar trees, hibiscus, oleander—and homes of every color—they reached the bustling metropolis. There they passed restaurants, boutiques, and multi-leveled pillared shops; much of the older architecture colonial in style. To their right the water shimmered in the harbour; sailboats and yachts drifting about.

They exited the bus in the middle of it all and Kylie and the girls headed down Front Street along the line of the harbour. A middle-aged man in a blazer and Bermuda shorts, dress socks pulled up to his knees, nodded a greeting as he crossed their path. Aside from such distinctive business attire, there was little notable difference between the natives and tourists; that is, without hearing their accent, which was often a blend of British and Bermudian descent, with some Portuguese.

Crossing the main street together, holding hands, they entered one of the many alley-like streets that intertwined between and behind the tall buildings of the main street. After an hour of perusing sundry shops, they lunched at an Italian restaurant with a brick wood-burning pizza oven as its centerpiece. The children always enjoyed sitting at the granite counter top, watching the chef scoop up the bubbling pizzas on lifters before sliding them onto pans.

No sooner had they begun to eat when Mya

reminisced about the last time they'd been here "with Daddy." Kylie bore it patiently for a few minutes before diverting the conversation elsewhere, thinking perhaps it was time to try a new restaurant; to make new memories.

She frowned at the thought. New memories or the obscuring of old?

They arrived back at the estate early afternoon and the girls changed into swimsuits while Kylie took a two-minute power nap in her own room, longing to sleep the afternoon away. She willed herself to stand up however, and changed into a bikini with a wrap-around pareo skirt, retrieving her sun hat as well. The girls ran ahead across the yard, beach towels under their arms flapping in the wind. Kylie chuckled as she followed them from a distance, pulling her hat down over her short curls.

Her brother leaned against a stone railing on the far side of a flagstone terrace which led off from the library. Staring off at the ocean, cigarette in hand, he seemed oblivious to the echoing laughter of his nieces, who were already splashing about in the shallows. Urns brimming with flowers adorned the four corners of the terrace. In the center was a cedar table with a lime parasol.

"Trey," she called out, waving as she

approached. He glanced in her direction and gave a nod. "When did you start smoking?" She cocked her head.

He looked back toward the sea with a slight scowl.

Deciding not to bother with him, she left the terrace and continued to the beach, making herself comfortable on a reclining chair. She pulled sunglasses and a magazine from her tote bag and set about to reading. Keira built a sand castle, decorating it with twigs, while Mya doggy-paddled; hair slick and shiny. Palm trees outlined themselves in shadow on the sand but the sun beat down on Kylie, making her sleepy again.

Far off to the right of the beach and nearly out of sight from where she reclined, stood the tennis court. It was vacant. Had Pearl and Ramiro gone to town together after playing; or parted ways? She pictured them heading outside after breakfast, chatting comfortably and swinging their rackets at their sides, crisp white towels draped over their shoulders. Ramiro would have a strong arm, on par with Pearl's own athletic skill. An energetic game would ensue, the ball flying over the net in soaring arcs, back and forth, back and forth. The whack of the racket making contact, the scuffing of sneakers. Ramiro took a high swipe, Pearl followed through with an underhand. She paused to dab her towel around her neck while he took a swill from a bottle of water . . . Ramiro Airoso . . . sun glistening on his handsome face as he removed his visor to wipe the sweat from his brow. The game resumed, his muscles straining beneath a taut shirt as he took a slow motion swipe at the ball—

Kylie blinked sharply and flipped the page in her magazine. Heat crept up her neck. What was she doing? It wasn't like her to fantasize about a man like that.

At least, not anyone besides Drew.

At teatime, Kylie accepted a shortbread cookie from Connie and nibbled at it. It was sweet and flaky, decadent, but this she noticed only vaguely and with little appreciation. After two bites, she set it down. No one else had attended tea and the library seemed cold and quiet, despite the happy chatter of the girls while Connie fawned over them. Edward was expected home by suppertime. It couldn't arrive soon enough—he was the pulse of the home.

Kylie sipped her tea without tasting it.

Mya asked if she could call her dad to say hi, but Kylie wasn't up to speaking to Drew and told her to wait until later. After all, they'd just called him the night before.

Finishing off her tea, she stared at the bookshelves.

At five-thirty her father arrived, his booming voice greeting Connie in the front entrance. Kylie jumped to her feet, gathered up the girls, and hurried them out into the hallway.

Edward Patterson gaped at the unexpected sight of his approaching daughter and grandchildren. "Why, Kylie—of all things!" He beamed, engulfing her in a beefy-armed embrace. She kissed his cheek and moved away so he could hug the children as well.

"When did you get here?" he asked breathlessly, blue eyes luminous above folds of skin.

"Yesterday afternoon," she said, smiling and relaxing. "We wanted it to be a surprise."

He glanced around then, a question forming in his eyes.

"No, he's not here."

He nodded, expression fading for a second, perhaps with disappointment. "A man can always hope, can't he?" He winked at her and put an arm around Mya. "I liked that chap—a most excellent golfing buddy. Come," he said, "we've much to discuss. I want to know all about the past year, how you've been, what you've been up to, all the good stuff."

He led them into a sunken sitting room next

to the foot of the staircase. Kylie crossed the pegged floorboards (intended to resemble the deck of a ship) and sat on the edge of a Victorian chaise lounge, clasping her hands together over her skirted knees. Mya examined an intricate model ship on a nearby stand while Keira sat down beside her grandfather on a brocade settee. Fishnet curtains on each of the sash windows were pulled aside and looped through metal rings.

Edward leaned back and exhaled noisily, his waist spilling over his Bermuda shorts and threatening to pop his shirt buttons. He'd made his fortune years ago and having no patience for idleness, always had to be doing something to keep himself occupied and amused. Though old enough to retire, he had no desire to; thriving on work and enjoying his leisure time all the more because of it. He also had clients in St. George and enjoyed spending a night or two there from time to time, to golf and fine dine with his good buddies.

He draped an arm over the back of the settee, his many rings glinting in the sunlight that filled the room. He chatting with his granddaughters, teasing and getting the giggles going. Kylie watched, smiling along. He used to be like that with her too, as a girl. But when her parents divorced during her teens, she moved to Canada with their mother, who soon remarried, and Trey stayed in Bermuda. He was eight years old at the time—seven years younger than Kylie due to an unplanned pregnancy—and their mother could have insisted on taking him too. But she decided to leave him with Edward instead; a decision Kylie would always find difficult to understand.

As time passed, Kylie adapted to her father's absence in their new life and felt content enough to chat with him on Skype between visits. It had been two years now since her last trip. He always insisted on paying their airfare but he'd never been off the Island himself to visit her in Canada, and likely never would. If she wanted to see him, she had to come here.

His curly hair receded at the temples and only a few highlights remained to suggest the color it had once been. His goatee was fully gray. Both Kylie and her brother had inherited their father's brunette curls, and little Keira in turn had inherited Kylie's. Edward's nose was bulbous and marred with capillaries, but he had a friendly smile. She'd never thought of her father as handsome, though in some ways his homeliness was part of his charm; and she sometimes wondered at Pearl's motives for being with him. It was easy to assume she'd preyed on him solely for his money but that seemed too

Hollywood classic to be true. Was this teddy bear, whom Kylie loved with all her heart, really the sort of man who kept a trophy wife? He was charismatic . . . affectionate. And despite his fondness for jewellery, unpretentious.

"So, sweetheart," he said suddenly, interrupting her reverie like a pat on the back, "tell me what's new in your life."

With the girls present, she didn't want to get too personal, so instead began talking about Mya's completion of grade one and Keira's excitement to begin Kindergarten in the fall. Safe territory.

"And why do you want to stay half the summer?" he asked after a while, changing the subject. "You're more than welcome, as you know, but it's a much longer stint than your usual."

She hesitated, trying to think of a satisfactory answer, but didn't really have one. Nor did she wish to mention her depression in front of the kids. Two weeks would have been more than enough for a tropical vacation, it was true, but it wasn't long enough to . . . to what?

Hurt Drew?

"It's been a difficult year for me, Dad." She looked up, shrugged. He could infer the rest.

"Are you still—?" He glanced at the girls, trailing off.

"Yes. He has an apartment."

"Going to uh, file?" He cleared his throat to muffle the word.

"I don't know yet."

"Ach, who am I to give romantic advice anyway?" He chortled, loosening his collar and tie. "I've been 'living in sin' for five years now, and have no intention of changing that. I don't want any woman feeling that she's stuck with me, like your mother did. If she wants to go, she can go—no paperwork to slough through, no money quarrels." A pointed look. "And if she stays, it's because she wants to, not because she has to." He began to sing a Sinatra tune, eyes twinkling. "Nice and easy does it . . . nice and easy does it,"—he whistled the instrumental line between, getting the kids laughing—"nice and easy does it . . . every time." He hummed the ending strain. Then, pulling himself to his feet, he patted his belly. "Well everybody, I need to unpack my suitcase before dinner, so I will see you again in about fifteen minutes—deal?" He kissed each one of them and left the room.

Kylie lay back on the chaise lounge and propped herself up on her elbow. She talked with Keira, who was flipping through a storybook and asking random questions, as Kindergartners do. Mya fiddled with a half-completed jigsaw puzzle on a nearby games table; letting out an exclamation of triumph each time she found the right piece.

Several minutes passed by before Kylie realized she was daydreaming about Pearl's handsome cousin, Ramiro.

She tried to clear her thoughts but he lingered.

CHAPTER 5

Later that evening after the children had gone to sleep, Kylie sat down with her father in the library to have some decaf tea, which he served her himself. Surprisingly, Pearl hadn't joined them for supper that night, though as it turned out, she'd been home since lunchtime—unbeknownst to all. Apparently she'd hurt her back playing tennis and was laid up in bed.

Edward removed a Cuban cigar from a cedar box on the end table next to his chair, cut off the tip and lit it. He puffed thrice and exhaled. The room soon became redolent of tobacco, a sweet savor Kylie found cozy and comforting, though she didn't smoke herself. He leaned back in the wing chair and crossed one ankle over his knee. Kylie sat in the other chair.

"How's Trey been lately?" she asked. He hadn't joined them for supper either.

"Oh the usual, I'd say." He smoothed his goatee a couple of times, looking contemplative. "Keeps to himself and never looks you in the eye—so who knows what he's up to these days." A laugh. "He comes, he goes and he just . . . " A toss of the hand.

"He didn't seem happy to see me yesterday," she said. "Even though it's probably been a good half year since we've Skyped. And at breakfast it was like pulling teeth just to start a conversation with him. He seemed . . . I don't know, sullen."

Edward scrunched his furry eyebrows together and puffed on the cigar.

She sipped her tea.

"I'm not sure," he said after awhile, "it's hard to say. It could simply be that he's too old to be living at home now and wants his privacy. I'm sorry to have to admit this to you, but I don't know the boy very well—never have. We've always kept ourselves busy for the most part, even when he was young. I figured he preferred it that way."

Edward rose from his seat to pour a glass of scotch from the nearby sideboard. He then switched on the stereo, keeping the volume low, and returned to his seat. The subject seemed to have subdued him; he looked pensive. She waited, hoping he'd say more about it. After a few minutes of mutual reverie he recalled a humorous anecdote from his day and shared it with enthusiasm. He seemed relieved to have thought of something amusing and superficial to discuss, and the mood lightened. She wondered if he'd eventually ask about Drew again, now that the children weren't there, but he didn't—and she wasn't about to bring it up herself.

Around eleven they said goodnight and she went to bed, leaving the curtains open to let the breeze in. Moonlight filled the room, accentuating both the pillows and the pastel quilt. She lay on one side of the double bed rather than the center, and stared at the fluffed pillow next to her. The space materialized with Andrew: lying there with his back to her, sleeping. Short black hair against the bone white of the pillow, the strong curve of his bare shoulder, the soft intake of his breath. She reached for him, nuzzling her nose in his hair at the nape of his neck, breathing in his scent . . . feeling the warmth of his body in the crook of her own. He stirred, tucking her arm under his and holding her hand against his chest. She drifted off to sleep.

He isn't there in the morning.

After a breakfast of bacon and eggs, Edward

departed for the day to his office in downtown Hamilton, Pearl went to her room, and the children went off to the library to watch cartoons. Kylie lingered at the dining table alone with a cup of coffee —this one with sugar.

It rained a little and the room was dim, almost drab despite its ornate finishes. Edward had left the morning paper on the table and Kylie flipped through it without really seeing.

At a quarter to ten, she was pouring herself a second cup of coffee when footsteps sounded in the hall. Trey and a plump young woman with long sandy hair entered the dining room and sat down across from her.

"Good morning," she said, smiling at the girl with veiled curiosity and focusing back on her brother.

Acknowledging the question in her eyes, he nudged a glance at the girl and said, "Cassidy."

"Hello, I'm Kylie. It's nice to meet you."

"Yeah thanks. Hi. You too." A groggy voice and a half smile, eyes peering out through cartoon-length lashes.

Connie entered the room from the kitchen, bringing the two newcomers a plate of reheated food. They accepted with mumbled thank-yous. Cassidy reached for her mug with glittery fingernails and lifted her gaze, looking from Kylie to Trey and back again.

"You look like him," she said, dumping two scoops of sugar and a dollop of cream into her mug.

Kylie grinned. "No—he looks like me."

Trey tittered and Cassidy elbowed him, laughing.

He cracked a smile.

They made small talk for a brief while, Trey as quiet as ever. When the conversation waned, Kylie decided it was time to take her leave. Small talk wasn't her forte either. She folded the newspaper, said her good-byes, and went to the music room after first checking on Mya and Keira.

In the corner next to a striped settee was her childhood violin, perched on a stand.

She picked it up and sat down, stroking the glossy maple wood with affection and reverence, running her fingertips over the strings. Retrieving the bow, she placed the instrument under her chin and began to play. It was a mournful tune, later merging into an intense classical piece and spiriting her away to a place all her own where she could express herself freely and with abandon.

After twenty minutes or so she became aware of someone watching her, and ceased playing with an abruptness that echoed through the room like a gong.

Ramiro Airoso stood in the open doorway, leaning against the frame with his sandaled feet crossed at the ankles.

"Oh please do not stop on account of me," he said with a grin. "It was stunning. I was quite enjoying myself."

She blinked at him as though waking from a deep sleep, and lowered the violin. "I should probably be checking on my kids," she said with an awkward laugh, standing up.

Rain trickled down the window panes and the room was in shadow. She put the violin back on the stand and switched on a lamp as Ramiro entered the room. He stood casually next to the grand piano, wearing khaki shorts and a silk shirt, damp on the shoulders; no doubt from being outside.

"You're very talented," he said. "Do you play professionally?"

She crossed her arms to keep from fidgeting. "Not in concert, no, though I'd love to some day. I'm a music teacher."

With a mischievous smile, he took a seat at the piano and splayed his fingers over the keys, his profile cast in shadow as he began to play.

It dawned on her after a short while of listening that he meant for her to play along. She reached for the violin again, heart racing as she sat down on the edge of the settee. Though tentative at first, she quickly grew confident as the two instruments blended together.

It was over all too soon.

"You play very well," she said breathlessly when he finished and pivoted on the seat to face her. A flush warmed and mantled her cheeks.

He grinned. "I am a man of many secrets, you might say." His eyes danced.

They went out into the hallway just as heels clicked on the staircase, descending, and Pearl appeared at the base.

The look she gave them was dark and grave, as though displeased, but she said nothing; instead heading for the front door and dawning a raincoat with a belted waist. She collected her purse and stood waiting, presumably for Ramiro.

"You'll have to excuse us," he said to Kylie, touching his hand to the small of her back before walking around her to go to Pearl. A tingle ran up her spine.

She moved forward and rested her hand on the newel post, watching them with what she hoped was a pleasant expression. Ramiro gave a nod good-bye and went out onto the portico—rain splattering the walkway beyond. The scent of wet grass filled the entranceway.

Pearl looked back over her shoulder as she

crossed the threshold. "I am going to run a few errands and will see you at dinner time, Kylie," she said, her smile plaster-like rather than genuine. She shut the door behind her.

Later that night after dinner, Edward and the girls played Go Fish and Old Maid in the living room and Kylie was left alone for the time being. She'd already joined them for several rounds and that was enough for her: they might play ten more times before calling it quits. Pearl retired to bed immediately after dinner saying she was under the weather, and indeed looked it.

On impulse, Kylie donned a windbreaker over her shorts and tee, and went outside through the French doors in the library. It was a foggy night. She headed down the slope toward the beach, grass slippery beneath her sandals, air damp and heavy. Pausing, she took a moment to look back at the house before continuing. The chimneys and con-tours formed a vague substance, the house fully enrobed in fog; flower urns and patio furniture like stains in the mist.

She took careful steps on the beach to avoid getting sandy feet, and the sea came into sight through the haze. Waves broke upon the shore with a roar, running back across the sand with a swish.

On second thought, she slid her feet from the sandals and went to the water's edge. The next wave approached and cold water tore around her ankles, rising almost to her calves and slipping away again. She closed her eyes and imagined herself being dragged out to sea . . . pulled underneath into that liquid onyx . . . ceasing to exist.

Goosebumps rose on her skin and she hugged her arms around her waist, staring ahead at the water. The spray from nearby rocks misted her face and curls.

In times past the sheer vastness and mystery of the sea inspired awe in her heart toward the Creator who'd made it; the only One who knew every single creature abiding in its endless depths. These days if she allowed thoughts of God to linger it left her feeling guilty. He wanted her to forgive. But she couldn't . . . at least not entirely.

She first noticed signs that she and Drew were growing apart when Keira was nearing toddlerhood, and not just apart, but worlds apart: as they literally were now. She couldn't say when exactly the change began but there were certain memories from years prior—dim ones at best—which suggested the erosion began after Mya's birth.

Postpartum depression.

She could recognize it, name it, list the

causes and symptoms, but it made no difference. Label or no label, she hadn't been able to make it go away. She adored her daughters, loved them passionately, delighted to watch them grow and to share in their daily lives. But the relentless fatigue, the anxiety—the sadness that came with it in those early years. . . . On the one hand she was happier as a new mother than she'd ever been in her life; on the other, she was overwhelmed with all the suffering in the world, filled with fears and worries for the girls' futures, and worn out from childcare and teaching.

If there was one thing she'd learned in life it was that peaches had pits. All good things had an inverse; dishes had to be cleaned, clothes had to be washed, snow shovelled, gardens weeded.

She didn't mean to push him away.

It was more subtle than that.

Instinct led her to shelter her wounds rather than exposing them to potential salt. It was easier to fake a smile than to explain how much she was hurting. Easier to distract herself with activities than to take a nap—not wanting to be alone with her gloomy thoughts. Easier to hang out with friends and be superficial than to admit that her marriage relationship was struggling. Probably easier for Drew to read or pursue recreation with his buddies for the same reason, though he did try many times to get her talking about it. But she recoiled from the raw vulnerability it triggered, that feeling of being pulled into a black hole. She avoided going deep, putting it off each time, waiting for a better moment. And where once they'd taken impromptu walks to cafés and waterfronts, played tennis and gone to the movies, they now had to procure a babysitter well in advance. This too made it easier and cheaper to take turns going out with friends instead of each other.

Another wave crashed around her ankles, its coolness nipping her skin and echoing the chill in her heart.

Early on she was aware of him trying to reach out to her: encouraging her to trust him and to share what she was going through. But her habit from late childhood had been to pick up the violin whenever feeling troubled, playing either a melancholy piece or an angry one, depending on her mood. It was cathartic, relieving her discomfort; at least for a while any way. So whenever communication with Drew felt strained, she knew of no other way to manage the tension. Why articulate arduous words when they flowed fluidly from the bow?

Yet when she was finally beginning to feel like herself again, when recovery was in full view—

she'd adapted to motherhood, no longer floundering—she discovered her husband had betrayed her.

With a shiver, Kylie turned around and picked her way carefully across the beach to where she'd left her sandals, grabbing them by the straps. The house came into focus as she approached the terrace. An upper bedroom window, her father's room, was suffused by lamplight, silhouetting a woman's form in its frame.

Pearl.

Kylie paused on the grass and stared at the window. Had Pearl been watching her the entire time?

The curtain fell in place, blanking out the light.

Shivering again, she entered the library and locked the French doors.

It was time to get the girls ready for bed and give Drew an obligatory phone call. Her stomach twisted at the thought.

CHAPTER 6

At nine o'clock, once the girls were in their pajamas and their teeth brushed, Kylie phoned her husband using the extension in her bedroom. Mya and Keira waited cross-legged on the bed, bouncing a little, eager to talk to their father.

He answered on the first ring.

"Hi," she said, heartbeat picking up a notch.

His strong tenor voice still had the power to move her; but his tone was guarded now, reserved, where once it had been warm and relaxed. She imagined him sitting on a leather sofa—her imaginary setting for him having a dreamlike quality. She hadn't been in his apartment, didn't want to see it, and preferred to think of him as just being at his brother's house. Maybe his absence would one day prove to be nothing more than a dream as well.

"Here's Keira," she said.

"Kylie, wait—"

She hesitated, holding the phone an inch from her ear and brought it close again. "Yes."

"How . . . are you?" His voice had softened.

A fluttering started in her chest. She groped for words. "I'm—fine."

"I miss you." His voice was barely a whisper.

Tears sprang to her eyes and she blinked them away, pivoting on the bed so the girls couldn't see. "Here's Keira—" She passed the phone off to her youngest daughter and went to the window, drawing aside the curtain.

Fog hovered low over the grass, waves rolling back and forth on the beach.

It was back in March when she asked— rather, told—Drew to leave.

He stayed with his brother, expecting it to be a short duration, but after a few weeks she confessed that she wasn't prepared to take him back anytime soon. His brother's basement apartment was vacant, so Drew insisted on renting it rather than wearing out his welcome in the guest room. He left most of his possessions behind at the house though, taking with him only a duffel bag full of clothes; making it clear that he still hoped it was a temporary situation.

After this they generally texted each other

only as it pertained to the children. Granted, he did send numerous messages those first few weeks pleading with her to discuss their separation. But she ignored and evaded all personal messages and questions, eventually telling him to stop asking: she would initiate when she was ready. How could she tell him what her plans were when she didn't know them yet herself?

In person there was nothing to do but act like virtual strangers—he with a lost puppy expression half the time and gravity the other—while she was a steady block of ice. Initially he tried to embrace her a few times, perhaps hoping affection would help, but she endured the hugs stiffly and did not return them. They told the children very little about the situation, only the basics, and struggled to answer their questions in age-appropriate ways; procrastinating on having to explain things in greater detail. Until a decision was made, what more could be said to them?

Of course he'd apologized profusely, dozens of times, and though she could forgive well enough, she wasn't going to act as if it were thus nothing of consequence. Forgiveness alone wasn't enough to fix things anyway; it didn't erase the pain, or solve the problem. As much as she wished they could go back to how it was before, what assurance did she have that it wouldn't happen all over again?

She felt frozen in place. Neither able to retreat nor move forward.

The memory of his betrayal haunted her in the face of every beautiful woman on TV, on every magazine cover, on every street, in every mall.

After Mya had her turn and disconnected the phone, Kylie took the children to their bedroom and read them several storybooks before tucking them in with a kiss and their favorite stuffed animals. She hesitated out in the hallway, considering whether to retire early for the night or to seek out her father's company. With an urge for a hot drink, her decision was made and she went downstairs.

After making a tea, she found her father in the library nursing a tumbler of scotch.

His tie had been removed and the top buttons of his shirt undone, revealing a mass of curly hair. He smiled at her but his gaze was far away. The dome of light over his wing chair from the lamp beside it was the only lighting in the room, so she switched on a second lamp before sitting down.

He focused on her more clearly then, blinking, and set down the now empty tumbler. "I'm off to St. George's tomorrow morning, unfortunately," he said, clearing his throat. "It's been the plan for quite a few weeks actually, otherwise I'd reschedule. Couple buddies of mine are getting together for some boating and golfing." His voice was thick. "I'll be staying at Lightbourne's place—you remember him, yes?"

Her heart sank at the thought of him leaving, but she kept her expression neutral.

"I'll be back by Saturday though," he said, as if sensing it when he met her eyes. "Will that be alright, sweetheart? I hate to strand you like this."

"It's no problem, Dad," she lied, "we'll make do. I didn't expect you to be waiting on me hand and foot." She feigned a cheery smile, not wanting him to see her disappointment.

He nodded and hefted himself up to a standing position. She thought he was going to leave but instead he took his tumbler to the liquor cabinet for a refill. He returned to his seat. "I'm sorry Pearl isn't more hospitable," he said in a confidential tone. "She's been reclusive for some time now, truth be told."

Kylie hesitated, choosing her words. "Has she been . . . unwell?"

He stared down at his tumbler, swirling the amber contents. "Maybe. But I'm not certain." He took a sip and leaned back in the chair. "I have noticed a few unusual things here and there . . . though nothing I can quite put a finger on. Half the time I figure she's merely bored of my company." A chortle escaped his lips. "Not that I blame her. Five years is a long time to stick around with a fat old toad like me."

Ramiro came to mind, along with his tendency to visit while her father was out.

"She loves you though?"

A brief pause. "You know I once thought so, she really had me convinced. But nah, not likely. I mean, not really anyway. At least, no more than I love her." Another laugh.

Kylie shifted in her chair, heat prickling her cheeks. "Then, why . . . ?"

He looked up at her with a grimace. "Isn't it obvious?"

She understood and for the moment hated him. Sure, she'd always figured as much, but to have him actually say so out loud felt like a punch in the throat.

"You men are all the same!" She stood so quickly she nearly spilled her tea as she plunked it down on the coffee table and fled the room.

"Kylie—"

Reaching the washroom, she locked herself inside without turning on the light and sat on the closed toilet seat lid, trembling.

First her husband, now her father.

She groped for a Kleenex and dabbed at her

eyes, refusing to let the tears drop out. She was too angry to cry. For the past few months she'd been trying to piece together the shards of her self-esteem and had made little progress. Now this. She would go straight to the music room and pick up the violin if it weren't for the time of day. But all she could do now was breathe deeply and wait for the nausea to subside.

After a few minutes of concentrated effort, numbness began to soothe her heart.

She left the washroom and ascended the staircase; the moon through the window above the front door a glowing smudge behind clouds. She checked on the girls and went to bed with a familiar ache in her throat; the waves on the beach lulling her to sleep.

They'd been gone half a week.

It felt like a month.

Something about his wife and children being far away on an island made time stand still. He couldn't drive across town and knock on their door anymore—he'd have to literally board an airplane and fly over the ocean to see them.

It was nine-thirty now, ten-thirty where she was. He wondered what she was up to and wished she would talk to him on the phone; at least give him a chance to say something before handing the phone to the children. Even when she let him visit the kids at the house on weeknights, she often left when he arrived and didn't return until he was ready to go—that or stayed in a different room. All the text messages he sent received a superficial response, if any response at all, and he could only conclude that she wanted nothing more to do with him. But if she wanted a divorce, why not just say so? Why the constant evasion? He hoped it was because she hadn't made up her mind yet. Still, it couldn't continue much longer this way, living in limbo like this. It wasn't fair to the children.

Those first tumultuous weeks of separation had gradually stretched into months—the longest four months of his life—and still he waited, hoping for a chance to turn things around, to reconcile.

But he was scared.

Deeply scared.

Almost to the point of despair. He didn't want a divorce—he still loved her.

And how he missed her, how he ached to hold her, to share a laugh and a smile . . . to simply be friends again. To be a family again.

Drew flicked through the cable channels one last time and shut off the small TV, tossing the remote onto the dinged-up coffee table he'd bought at a thrift shop for five bucks. Nothing worth watching. He picked up a golfing magazine from the stack on the table and scanned the table of contents.

When he was twenty-one, he took a dream vacation to Bermuda with his older brother, Joel. They were both avid golfers and thought Bermuda would be the perfect place for a tropical vacation. And so it was. It was also where he first met Kylie.

He and Joel were swimming at Horseshoe Bay Beach, named for its shape: a rounded swath of blushing sand with towering outcrops on one side and cozy coves on the other.

The beach was crowded, being an especially hot day, and wanting a break from the noisy throng, Drew had gone to explore a cove on the far end of the beach. Ducking into the sequestered area, he found it empty, save for a young woman sitting on a boulder; her feet in the water and a sun hat hiding her face from view. She wore a pareo skirt over her lemon-colored bikini and had pretty little legs, tanned and glinting in the sunshine.

His first instinct was to retreat and not disturb her privacy but she looked toward him, removing her hat.

"Hello," she said with a smile, running her hand through chocolately curls and setting her hat on her knee. "Gorgeous day, isn't it?"

He grinned and glanced up at the sky. "Sure is." He gave her a second look, half-shy, and seeing no ring on her hand, decided to plunk down on a nearby rock. The translucent water was about two inches deep here, cool and refreshing. He stuck out a hand and gave hers a shake. "Name's Andrew."

She smiled again, a fleeting dimple in her cheek suggesting a merry disposition. "I'm Kylie."

Her eyes were gentle and friendly, the irises an Arctic blue, like a husky's. She had a small nose and a delicate chin. He thought she was the prettiest girl he'd ever seen.

They talked about the Island and its particular features, and soon got to talking about the golf courses. It was then he learned she was from Ontario too. A moment of startled delight followed this discovery, a slow grin spreading across his lips and then across hers in turn. They were both thinking the same thing—had to be. On a whim, he invited her to join him for lunch and they left the cove and sauntered across the beach, maneuvering around sunbathers and pointing out this and that to one another. He introduced her to his brother when they came upon him, and continued to the beach café, a teal building with a layered limestone roof. They sat at a patio table outside enjoying fries and iced tea.

When it was time to part ways, they made arrangements to get together again the next day.

Over the week that followed, they saw each other three more times: the final time at Kylie's father's estate, where she invited him and his brother for the afternoon. His attraction was so clearly mutual that there wasn't any insecure moment of wondering whether or not he was moving too quickly. And knowing she felt the same, he kissed her for the first time in the shade of a fifteen-foot tall Bermuda palmetto at the side of Edward Patterson's house.

They continued to date exclusively in Ontario, living only two hours apart. Six months later they returned to Bermuda for a week at her father's home and Drew proposed to her under the moongate leading into the garden. A fairytale romance if ever there was one.

Now, ten years and two children later, was this the end?

If he could turn back the clock, he'd smash his computer into a thousand pieces instead of clicking that link.

CHAPTER 7

Drew whipped the golf magazine back onto the coffee table, knocking the remote to the floor. He hated that memory.

It happened a year ago.

Though he'd known Kylie was depressed, she didn't like to talk about it. And once in a moment of exasperation he'd asked her why she couldn't just be happy. After that she'd withdrawn all the more.

For a time he was ticked. Why did she block him when all he wanted to do was help, to cheer her up? They'd been best friends from the get-go and now she was shutting him out, retreating into herself. Eventually it seemed only Mya and Keira were capable of bringing a genuine smile to her face, a light to her eyes. He couldn't help feeling like it was all his fault, like he wasn't good enough anymore.

In the early years after having children, their lovemaking at times felt mechanical; she seemed apathetic. He figured it was fatigue, he felt it too; but it still hurt. The children had them up a lot in the night, especially during their infancies, so it was understandable. But he couldn't make her depression go away, and coped by filling his timetable to keep distracted; trying to be patient but brooding more than he cared to admit. Eventually his Christian faith moved him to forgive and dig up that bitter root. Not forgiving her for her depression though—he didn't blame her for that—but rather for shutting him out when all he wanted to do was help. Forgiveness hadn't been enough though: the gap left behind, from letting go of resentment, made the loneliness and anxiety feel all the more keen. He ached for a tonic.

The first time he clicked a link, he told himself he'd only clicked it by accident.

A twitch of a nerve in his finger.

He hadn't intentionally meant to see anything but his pulse was racing and breathing shallow. It took quite a few minutes of gazing at the collage in front of him before he mobilized himself to close the website. Then he sat back and stared at the blank screen for a full half hour until his heart-beat slowed down to normal again.

He hadn't done this since his late teens; repented of and abandoned before he even met Kylie. And for nearly a decade he'd believed marriage was the cure for such temptations.

That night Kylie was asleep on her side and facing the wall when he crawled into bed. With a knot in his stomach, he prayed for forgiveness, explaining to God how it was only a mistake and he didn't mean to do it. He put his arm around Kylie's waist and his nose into the curls on her neck, breathing in the lovely scent: mandarin oranges. He closed his eyes and like a jolt, the images were as vivid as if they'd been scorched into his retinas.

When he first married, his love for Kylie had suppressed all the imagery from his teen habit and it took little effort to keep it out of mind. But that night he'd gone and supplanted Kylie.

Never would he forget the juxtaposition of horror and longing that filled his being in that moment. The irrevocable nature of what he'd done, and the longing to see more.

Two full weeks passed before he did it again.

He was in a mood. Anxious. Tired, lonely, sad. The usual queue. He wondered if this was what depression felt like for Kylie. He was bored too. The girls were asleep, Kylie was out with friends and wouldn't be home for a couple of hours, nothing on TV. He juggled the desire for a full hour, heady, pulse racing, trying to rationalize himself out of it. Eventually it seemed safe enough to go online and look at golfing websites.

That lasted all of ten minutes.

One minute he was looking at a golf course, the next he was deliberately blocking his conscience and letting himself feel only his desires. If he allowed himself to think for even one second he'd be guilt-ridden. So he focused on what he felt instead: a raw emptiness in the core of his being. Like a hollow ache in the chest when one misses a couple of meals, or the dry parched sensation after hours spent in the sun. In that moment he allowed himself to feel instinct only: ravenous, salivating instinct. With one drop of water on the tongue two weeks prior, how could he not now chug back the entire contents of the glass?

After that, despite miserably repenting to God each time it happened, piling excuses to the sky, he found himself indulging on a weekly basis.

Eventually it was twice a week . . . then every other day . . . sometimes daily.

Stomach cramping, Drew quashed the

memories and went to his room, flopping down on the bed. He pressed his face into the blanket, heart heaving in his chest. Oh, God, how he despised himself. Why why why did he trade his very wife —the love of his life—for nothing more than images on a screen?

And what a year that had been—living a double life. Him, desperately hiding his secret; Kylie, growing ever more suspicious, pestering him, asking pointed questions, nagging. She wanted to know why he didn't go out with his friends as often as before, why he seemed to jump at the chance every time she wanted to go out with hers; why he'd be so petulant out of nowhere. Sure, they both had their share of moodiness before that, especially due to the growing strain between them, but now he was fussing and snarling over the most trivial and benign things. He figured for a while she probably thought he was having an affair. But as time passed without detection, he grew too bold, sometimes daring to log on even when she was home, though always deleting his trail.

Then that final night—when he thought her asleep—a footfall sounded behind him on the carpet.

It was almost a relief to be caught.

But also like death.

He begged her to forgive him, pleaded with

her, but she refused to discuss it, wouldn't even hear him out. Not that night nor any other. Those husky-blue eyes he loved so much were cold as Alaska. She caught him on a Wednesday night, and by Saturday morning he capitulated and packed a duffel bag; driving to his brother's home to stay in the guest room. He confessed all to Joel—likely his saving grace. If not for that accountability he might have stop-gapped his anguish by gorging more than ever, a dog returning to his vomit. But Joel took the protective place of friend and brother, providing the support and encouragement he needed. They'd always been close; if only he'd had the courage to confide in his brother sooner though, instead of when it was no longer a choice.

He went for counselling by himself at first, hoping Kylie would soon join him for couple's therapy, but she refused. He continued going on his own. If she ever let him talk about it, he'd tell her how he was working through the issues that led him to use and how he had no intention of using again. Yes, he did have a few slip-ups early on after starting counselling—when he realized the separation might lead to divorce—but these slip-ups soon prompted him to take the additional step of installing blocking software on his computer, with reports sent to Joel. Knowing that his addiction had been self-medication for anxiety and loneliness—now exacerbated by the loss of his wife—he searched for a healthy alternative. He settled on jogging, which was easy to fit into his daily routine. After that he'd been able to stay on track. It wasn't a secret anymore, the secret being the strongest manacle. And he didn't want to sabotage his only hope by turning back to the very thing that had shackled his life in the first place—even if that meant using blocking software for the rest of his life, which he fully intended to do.

Drew clasped his fingers together behind his head, breathing into the blanket, half suffocating himself.

Could she ever love him again?

He rolled over onto his back and stared at the ceiling, silently crying out to God. God knew his heart, knew the depths of his agony and regret; in this he was fully confident. When words failed, it was enough just to turn his grieving spirit toward the Spirit of God. This communion was his only solace. Even spending various weeknights and every Saturday with his daughters could not set these broken arms. The time with Mya and Keira, nowhere near enough, was a heartaching comfort: he felt like a trespasser in his own home. There was a veil between them now, like the frosted glass of the light fixture on the ceiling above him—a grave-yard for bugs, a dead zone.

How long could he continue living in the twilight?

Kylie woke early Wednesday morning to the sun shining through the windows and the ocean shimmering in the distance.

After dressing in shorts and a tee, she helped Mya and Keira get ready for the day, and together they went downstairs for breakfast. Connie met them there and informed her they'd be dining on the terrace. Her father was already there at the head of the table, reading the newspaper.

He closed the paper as they approached and stood to greet the girls with kisses and bear hugs. Kylie too was engulfed in a hug before she could sit down at the table in a chair near him. Breakfast hadn't been served yet so she gave the girls permission to play on the lawn while they waited. It was ideal weather for a breakfast outside; a slight breeze to ruffle curls without blowing away napkins.

Kylie glanced into the library through the open French doors and turned back to her father, surprised to find him watching her.

He cleared his throat. "I'm sorry for what I said last night, sweetheart." His eyes were gentle, contrite. "I didn't mean to hurt you."

She looked down at the table, keeping her expression neutral. "If it's how you honestly feel, why apologize?" She met his gaze, this time letting her anger show. "The hurt is in the truth, not that you said it."

He narrowed his eyes thoughtfully and glanced toward the children. They were a good five meters away, sitting cross-legged on the grass, plucking blades and chattering with one another.

"We're beating around the bush, I suspect,"—he turned back to her—"because you haven't yet told me your own story. All this time I've been left to make my own conclusions. So tell me. Why did Andrew move out? You've always been a private person and I'm not one to pry. I figured you'd tell me when ready."

She startled, tucking a curl behind her ear to hide her embarrassment.

"He left because I told him to."

Edward knit his hands together over his paunch and leaned back in the chair. "Another woman?"

She didn't respond right away, instead looked out to the sea.

A gull swooped and dived on the horizon.

Connie emerged from the house then with a tray of tea things and orange juice, a welcome distraction. She poured a cup for Kylie, filled the girls' cups with juice, and set out an additional China cup and glass at the foot of the table, presumably for Pearl. After promising breakfast would be ready shortly, she left them alone.

Kylie fiddled with the handle of her cup but didn't lift it to her lips. Her father was waiting patiently for a response. She could feel him watching her, the side of her face tingling under the scrutiny. A breeze carried the tea's aroma to her nose and she felt hungry. Empty.

"It was porn." She met his eyes.

He didn't move or look away.

After what seemed an endlessly drawn out second, or handful of seconds, he spoke with a voice like a sigh. "My little girl . . . " A fold formed between his eyebrows. He put his palms on the table, smoothed the tablecloth. "Was he not sorry?"

"He was."

He smoothed his goatee.

"Dad, I don't expect you to understand." Even her closest friends thought her stance was too extreme. Her own mother thought it was ridiculous.

Gracious child, haven't you ever read an erotic novel?

It's not the same, Mom, these are real women.

Even still . . . it's not like he had an affair . . . it's different.

But it isn't different. Not to me.

"Why wouldn't I understand?" her father asked, interrupting her thoughts.

"Because for all I know, you do the same and think it's fine! Just like everybody else."

"What if I told you that I don't?"

"Then I'd say it's because you don't have to." She glanced into the library. "You have *her*."

He leaned back in his chair again. "Ahh. So that's it then. You think he did it because you weren't pretty enough."

She let out a clipped laugh, electricity coursing through her body. "Your girlfriend is a supermodel," she said, confident Pearl was nowhere nearby. "You told me last night"—she lowered her voice—"that you don't really love her. Yet you keep her. Whatever for if you don't love her? She's your living breathing playboy bunny."

Her father's eyes widened as though she'd slapped him. His mouth opened a crack but nothing came out.

Children's laughter lifted on the breeze and a butterfly flitted about the flowers in the urn next to the table.

He closed his mouth. Reaching for his tea cup, he lifted it to his lips; the cup outrageously tiny in his hand.

A sip. A swallow. Adam's apple bobbing. "I suppose it serves me right for what I said." Another sip and swallow. "I was dull with drink last night and feeling downright cynical." He leaned in, voice dropping to a confidential tone. "I think we both have our resentments, but you're wrong about Pearl. I do love her. Daft of me to suggest other-wise. Look, if you must know, I think I'm losing her —and it has me somewhat panicky. She could have any man she wants . . . what do I have to offer? So for you to call her a—well." He leaned back. "If you weren't my daughter, I'd be furious right now. Please don't disrespect Pearl like that again."

Footsteps sounded within the library and Pearl appeared a moment later at the open doors, Connie close behind with a breakfast cart.

Kylie stiffened, avoiding eye contact until she'd calmed down enough to be cordial; heart pounding.

CHAPTER 8

The children were called and everyone gathered around the table. At Pearl's request, Connie went into the library and turned on a Fado CD.

"Edward, will you say grace this morning?" Pearl asked with a sweet smile. She wore white slacks and a floral blouse; hair gathered into a coiled knot at the nape of her neck.

"Certainly." Everyone bowed their heads. "Our gracious heavenly Father," he began, "we thank thee for this bountiful meal that is set before us, ah-men."

Kylie's father wasn't a religious man, at least, not that he'd ever professed to anyone. She'd long ago assumed that saying a prayer before a meal was more of a tradition for him than a belief. When she first gave her heart to Jesus as a teen, she was eager to share her newfound faith with both parents, but they only seemed bewildered by her passion—wary—and not at all interested.

Gentle guitar strains swirled about them, intertwining with the sound of waves . . . the scraping of forks against plates . . . the crunch of toast.

Fado. Portuguese. She'd once researched the genre and learned that one of its common themes was a longing for someone lost or unattainable, a feeling sadder than nostalgia. Palpably: the presence of absence.

The presence of absence . . . a ghost in the house.

Drew.

Kylie blinked and glanced at Pearl.

Why did she love this music so much? Was it merely cultural or did she too long for something or someone never materializing on the horizon—or ever slipping away from sight over the shoulder?

Edward chatted with the boisterous children playfully as Kylie and Pearl sat in silence for most of the meal. Pearl didn't usually have a great deal to say anyway, likely an introvert. Or even a snob for that matter: deliberately taciturn with people who didn't amuse her.

Kylie feigned overt interest in spreading jam on her toast and watched the woman in her periphery. It came as no surprise that Pearl had forgone even one bite of bacon, taking only eggs and toast. Moving the spongy puffs around on her plate, nibbling here and there; eating her unbuttered toast with delicate bites. Was this how she maintained her figure? No, it had to be more than that. She was much too toned and athletic-looking for a regular exercize routine. And it certainly wasn't Edward utilizing the elaborate exercise room in the basement.

Kylie took a forkful of her own eggs, letting the buttery folds melt on her tongue before chewing.

"I have been told that your father is abandoning us for a few days," Pearl said without warning, sniffling. She reached into her pocket for a folded tissue and dabbed at her nose.

Kylie blinked. "Yes . . . but it's fine." She smiled a little. "There's plenty to keep us busy here." True enough, at least. "If the sunny weather continues I imagine we'll spend a lot of time on the beach."

A curt nod. Pearl reached for the teapot then and poured black tea into her cup, testing to make sure it wasn't scalding before taking a sip.

"You don't like milk in your tea?" The words came out before Kylie could stop them. Heat climbed her cheeks. Why say such a thing out loud? She was on a roll today.

Pearl set the cup down on its saucer so gently it made no clink, and lifted her large dark eyes to meet Kylie's. "I love milk." She lowered her sweeping lashes, lifting them again toward the sea. "I love bacon too." A sweet smile and resumed eye contact. "I envy you, Kylie. I wish with all of my heart that I too could eat all of these things and be petite." Not a single note of condescension laced her tone. She really meant it.

Kylie held back a guffaw. "I'd give up bacon in a heartbeat if I could look like you."

Pearl didn't laugh or act flattered in response, as might have been expected. Her expression remained sombre. "You and I ought to get to know one another better," she said, flicking an unreadable glance in Edward's direction. He was still being silly with his granddaughters, a natural child entertainer. Pearl picked up her tea cup and took a sip, the soul in her eyes looking as old as the sea reflected in them.

A cheerful Fado tune succeeded a dreary one and Kylie relaxed her shoulders, closing her eyes a moment as a cedar-scented breeze kissed her cheeks and collarbones.

They finished up breakfast and Edward bade his good-byes, soon on his way. Pearl excused herself and went upstairs, and for the rest of the morning, Kylie and the girls sunbathed on the beach, swimming intermittently.

Both Pearl and Trey were absent from lunch.

"Does Trey have a job?" Kylie asked Connie later that afternoon during tea time, wondering if this might explain his regular absences.

"No, ma'am," she answered, pouring a glass of juice for the children. "But he comes and goes as he pleases." A smile. "Speaking of which, here he is now." Kylie followed her gaze toward the hallway as the young woman named Cassidy entered the room, Trey in tow.

Cassidy wore an off-the-shoulder green shirt and black tights. She removed a ball cap, ponytailed hair flattened and damp beneath. "It's a scorcher out there," she said happily, plunking down on an armchair. She smiled at everyone, eyes half cloaked beneath fake lashes, giving her a sleepy look. Trey sat next to Keira on the sofa, resting one jean-clad ankle over his knee, foot twitching in a Converse shoe as he leaned back against the cushions. He looked bored and restless, eyes partially obscured by a shag of curls.

With his presence came the sickly-sweet scent of stale cigarette smoke.

"You stink," Keira said, wrinkling up her button nose and inching away from his side.

"Keira," Kylie whispered, "don't be rude."

Trey looked down at his niece but didn't alter his position. She blinked back up at him, eyes wide and mouth pursed. She looked at her mom, then at Connie, and back at Trey. "Well, he does," she said.

He looked away.

"It's true you know," Cassidy piped in, laughing and giving him a look of affection. "I'm afraid I'll get lung cancer just kissing you. Listen to your niece, yes?" She turned to Kylie. "I keep telling him to quit."

"Yeah, yeah," he mumbled. "Have your fun. I don't complain about that stupid tongue ring."

Cassidy stuck out her tongue at him, wiggling the barbell around. The girls squealed.

"Too much information," Kylie said with a laugh. "So tell me, how did you guys meet?"

Cassidy winked at Trey and he gave her a wry look in return. "Oh you'll never believe me. The library! I'm taking a two-year course to be a pastry chef, you see, and so there we were, downtown, sitting at the very same table together, a bunch of books open in front of us—and I happen to notice that his books were cookbooks just like mine. Mhm! Yup! So, I strike up a convo—he's so shy—you have to coax him a bit to get him out of his shell. But that was easy enough and soon we were whispering back and forth so loud he was getting embarrassed. He said 'let's go some place else,' and I was all for it. Totally inseparable since then.

"He does most of his cooking practise at my place, since he's not in school," she explained. "I give him free range of the kitchen, my parents don't mind it, and the deal is, he just has to clean up all his dishes after." A musical laugh. "Basically, he's leeching off my education 'cause I love to share. But there's something about teaching as you learn that helps it stick in your mind, you know? My focus is on desserts though, so he's already leaving me in the dust when it comes to entrées and stuff—but he does make one hel—one *heck* of a crème brûlée."

"Really? Trey does?" Kylie glanced at her brother in surprise.

A pink flush mantled his cheeks.

Cassidy nodded. "Like no one I've ever known. He's über talented."

Trey scoffed. "Not that great."

"What are you talking about? You're seriously the best cook I know."

"Can you cook something for us sometime?" Kylie asked with genuine interest, nodding toward the girls.

He met her gaze for the first time, blue eyes glinting white, like drifting glaciers.

"I don't think so."

"But why not if you're so good at it?"

He closed his eyes slowly, exhaling, as though the question required a great deal of tolerance to answer. "I'd just be in the way."

"But does Dad know you like to cook?"

He shook his head.

"Why not? I don't see why he wouldn't let you cook now and then. He'd probably enjoy a break from it. Does Pearl even cook on the nights when he works late?"

"I'd rather just cook at Cassidy's." He stood up and started for the door. "Anyways, time to jet, got some stuff to do. See ya 'round."

Cassidy followed suit, waving good-bye with an apologetic look. She replaced her ball cap as she walked, pulling the ponytail through the back.

After supper, the girls watched a children's movie in the library while Kylie spent an hour in the music room playing the violin. The room had originally been outfitted for her mother, who though an amateur pianist, had a penchant for music and was self-taught on several instruments. Kylie spent many hours practising the violin in this room as a child, eventually playing duets with her mother as well. After the divorce, Edward left the room as is, claiming it was because he wanted Kylie to keep using it whenever she visited. She figured it was more than that though; that he liked to remember how things once were and couldn't bear to change it.

With the violin beneath her chin, she looked toward the piano and thought of Ramiro Airoso, wondering if she might see him again. She wouldn't mind another duet. For many years she wished Drew had known a musical instrument and could join her. He did appreciate classical music though and they enjoyed several concerts together over the years—but to actually play music together . . . he might have learned to transpose the unsung words in her melodies. Then she wouldn't have had to try to say them out loud.

But it was too late for that now.

She made her choice and he made his.

The girls bounded into the room then, breaking her reverie and informing her that their movie was over. They bickered. She set the violin down with reluctance. It was time to get them ready for bed, and to let them phone their father.

Mya did the dialing and after enthusiastically sharing her day with him for several minutes, she said her good-byes and thrust the phone toward Kylie instead of Keira. "He wants to talk to you first, Mommy."

Kylie took the phone without lifting it to her ear, and went to the window overlooking the tennis court. It was awash in the lingering rays of sunset, soon to be engulfed in the shadows of dusk. Though she'd played the occasional game of tennis with Drew over the years, just now she remembered Ramiro in his tennis garb. Did he visit Pearl often? Was he single . . . married?

The receiver in her hand scalded and she nearly dropped it. How could she think of such things with her estranged husband on the line?

She lifted the phone, wondering if it might also scald her ear.

They exchanged preliminaries. He asked how her father and Pearl were, how Trey was. She answered each question with the basics, suppressing a tone of suspicion. Why the small talk? They hadn't been on confidential terms since the separation began and she wasn't about to resume now, on the phone.

"Why won't you talk to me?" he said suddenly. "I mean, really talk to me."

Her heartbeat quickened, a heady sensation coming over her. "This is hardly an appropriate time." She glanced at Mya and Keira who were sitting on the bed expectantly.

"Can I call you back later once the girls are asleep?"

"I don't think so."

"When is a good time then?" Strength entered his voice, a fervency—anger even. "You keep putting me off, months have passed, we've got to talk. . . . Can't you at least let me know your intentions?"

A gull swooped down and landed on the tennis court. It folded its wings and wandered about.

"There's nothing to talk about, Drew." She felt like a child then, instantly regretting her response. Nothing to talk about? More like where to begin.

A long pause followed. This wasn't the first time he'd asked to talk about what had happened. Whenever he did, she felt overwhelmed and flooded with emotion. That black hole again. Her kneejerk reaction was to stonewall, lest she lose the ability to stay calm. Usually he responded to her refusal with patience—though always notably disappointed and frustrated—but this time he sounded exasperated.

"I have to ask," he said finally. "Do you still love me?" He hadn't asked before.

A thousand answers raced to her tongue and died on the tip.

"I . . . don't know."

Silence. A bristling vacuum with a growing

charge.

She couldn't bear another second. "Here's Keira!"

Leaving the window, she handed the phone to her youngest daughter, hand trembling, and wished the child had already spoken to her father so she could just hang up. What a thing for him to ask over the phone, putting her on the spot like that. What did he expect? It was true though, she didn't know. She just didn't know anymore.

After putting the children to bed, Kylie picked a novel from the library and went to bed early to read; longing for a distraction from her troubled thoughts.

She awoke pre-dawn to the sound of vomiting.

CHAPTER 9

Thinking at first it was Mya or Keira, Kylie hurried from her bed and went out into the moonlit hallway to check on them.

More vomiting.

But it was coming from her father's room.

She knocked on the door. "Pearl? Are you okay?"

A light switched on from somewhere within, spilling out from the gap beneath the door.

"Pearl?"

Shuffling footsteps.

"I am fine," came a garbled voice. "I will be alright!"

"Is there anything I can do?"

"No, no—I am alright."

With a heavy exhale, Kylie returned to her room and grabbed her housecoat, pulling it on as she went downstairs. She paused at the music room, thirsting to pick up the violin; but not wanting to wake the household, she turned and went to the kitchen instead.

Opening the door, she stopped short before entering. Someone was hunched over the faintly-lit European range, wearing a chef's coat and working away, his back to her. He lifted his head at the sound of her footfall, casting a wide-eyed glance over his shoulder.

"Oh, Trey—it's you," she said with relief, approaching and pulling out a chair from the table in the center of the room. A waft of baking corn-bread filled her senses.

He frowned, looking displeased; a lock of hair fell downward, obscuring an eye. He returned to his work. Several cookbooks lay open in front of her. Kylie clasped her hands together on the table-top and pulled her chilly feet up onto the stretcher of the chair. She shivered. "Whatcha making?"

"Codfish Breakfast."

She glanced at the clock above the looming kitchen dresser, straining to see it in the pre-dawn shadows. "What time is it?" she asked, giving up. "It must be five or so."

"Four-thirty."

She leaned back. "Why are you cooking breakfast so early?"

"Gosh, Kylie!" He glared at her. "What are you even doing up?"

"I heard someone barfing and thought it was one of the kids, but it was Pearl. Listen—do you know what's going on with her? Has she only been sick for a few days?"

He added some onion to a sizzling, crackling pan, along with several strips of bacon. Her mouth watered as the delicious aroma grew strong and blended with the scent of the cornbread.

"Trey."

"What!"

"I asked if you knew what's wrong with Pearl."

He took a pot to the Belfast sink, switched on a light, and rinsed a handful of boiled eggs.

She was getting used to the back of his head. "So do you?"

An exaggerated sigh. "I don't give two f—"

She cut him off. "Have you at least noticed?"

He returned to the stove to pull out the cornbread, and set it on a cooling rack. "Seems the same to me as she's always been. Full of herself."

Kylie thought about this for a moment.

"How often does her cousin visit?" she asked.

"Cousin?"

"Yes, Ramiro."

He laughed. "Whenever Dad's not here."

A chill ran down her spine. The possibility had crossed her mind before but she'd hoped against it. "Does Dad suspect anything?"

Trey shrugged. "Who knows. We never talk." He set two plates on the table and scooped steaming codfish on each one, adding sauce and arranging eggs, sliced bananas, boiled potatoes, and a wedge of cornbread alongside the fish.

She recalled her conversation two night's ago with her father when he said that Pearl might have grown tired of him. He seemed dismissive too, attributing her disinterest to his size; laughing it off as if he didn't care. But yesterday he'd admitted to being genuinely worried about it. In previous years when Kylie visited, Pearl doted on him, showering him with attention and affection. His weight was the same then as it was now.

Trey sat down at the far end of the table, his mass of tumbling curls like a fedora in the shadowy light.

"This looks amazing, Trey, thanks for indulging me." She dug in. "Do you do this often—cook under the cloak of darkness?"

He tittered. "Only when Dad's away."

"When the cat's away, the mice will play." She met his eyes with a grin but he didn't smile back.

"What's with everyone doing stuff behind Dad's back anyway?" she continued. "He's a teddy bear—what are you afraid of?"

A scowl. "I'm not afraid of him, Kylie, I just don't feel like explaining myself to him all the time. He'll ask too many questions and be all up in my face in that infernal way of his. You know—when he's pushy with a big smile. Makes you feel guilty to hate it! And then he'll try an' take over an' manage the whole thing. . . . He'd have me enrolled in culinary school by sundown, if he knew."

"It's true, he's very hands-on about such things, isn't he." She raised an eyebrow. "Definitely a cheerful taskmaster."

"Yeah—and that's what makes it so, so—" He inhaled, cussed. "It's like the only time he notices me is when I do something impressive—or, or, annoying. Otherwise I'm just a ghost."

She nodded. "But are you against going to culinary school?"

He finished off his plate, pushed it aside. "I don't know." Chair legs scraped across the floor as he stood and gathered the dishes to be washed. "I haven't decided, and anyway, I don't want to be forced to, by anyone. It'll just take all the fun out of it."

She remembered her teen years when her father used to urge her to go further and further with the violin. At first she welcomed his interest in her passion but eventually it became stifling. There was a sense of guilt for not having achieved her dream of playing in an orchestra; a sense that she wouldn't have his full pleasure until that monumental day, should it ever come. Her father was an ambitious man and wouldn't have made his fortunes otherwise, but that same drive caused him to push others too hard sometimes, albeit always with such charm. He probably just saw himself as an enthusiastic supporter.

She rose and helped her brother with the dishes, wishing she'd worn slippers. The floor had locked in the cold of night. She shivered, glancing out the window where the first glow of sunlight silhouetted the palms.

"If you enjoy cooking so much," she said, "why not give school some serious consideration? Go because you want to go, not because Dad might suggest it. Then it's your idea not his. Just think—you could be a chef!"

He bristled visibly but said nothing. She let it go. Far be it from her to be pushy like her father. It'd be so much worse: she didn't have half his charm.

Pearl did not emerge from her bedroom until almost two o'clock in the afternoon when a knock came at the front door. It was Ramiro Airoso.

The girls had changed out of swimsuits after hours on the beach and were watching the flat screen TV mounted above the fireplace in the library. Kylie was on her way to the kitchen for a cup of coffee when the knock sounded. She opened the door and he walked right on in, looking very pleased to see her. She smiled and said hello, turning around to look at Pearl, who was already descending the staircase. Her smile faded.

Pearl stopped halfway down to steady herself, gripping the railing. She wore silk pajamas; plum leggings with a matching button down top. Her hair was dishevelled and she seemed groggy.

Ramiro adjusted the leather satchel on his shoulder and went to Pearl, taking her by the elbow tenderly, and brushing the hair out of her eyes. Kylie clasped her hands behind her back; thinking again of Trey's comment about Ramiro only visiting when Edward was away. Curious behavior for so-called cousins.

Pearl caught her gaze then with an almost childlike expression, though without makeup she looked older than usual. She said nothing but her eyes seemed to transmit a message, to be pleading. But pleading what though?

Rescue me? Or don't tell your father.

Probably the latter.

Irritated, Kylie turned on her heel and went into the kitchen to prepare a cup of coffee, casting furtive glances out to the hallway where a wedge of the staircase could be seen. She pictured Ramiro leading Pearl into that luxurious bedroom and then —no, stop it, don't think such thoughts. He said they were cousins and you have no proof to the contrary.

Her face felt hot and she grabbed at the sugar bowl on the table, knocking off the lid. She blinked. This was silly. Why should it matter what sort of relationship Pearl and Ramiro had?

Because of her father. Nothing more than that.

She put a scoop of sugar in her coffee, stirred, and reached for the lid to put it back in place as footsteps sounded on the stairs. She froze.

Next came footsteps in the hall, and Ramiro entered the room.

CHAPTER 10

Unbidden relief rushed through her. Relief? Yes, she must admit it. Five minutes was not enough time to . . .

"Pearl is resting now," he said. "She's not feeling well, as I'm sure you know." He seemed to hesitate then, as though considering something. "Would it be terribly forward of me to request another duet?" That knee-weakening smile.

Her heart skipped a beat but she tried not to look overly eager. "Not at all. That would be lovely." She abandoned her cup of coffee and they went to the music room. After she'd switched several muted lamps, Ramiro sat down at the grand piano and Kylie took a seat on the settee, lifting the violin to her chin.

For the next hour or so, they played one

piece after another. Beethoven's Kreutzer and Spring Sonatas, Chopin's Nocturne, Debussy's Violin Sonata. It was like a dream—exhilarating to play with an equally skilled musician. He played beautifully, and knew every piece she requested.

They finished the last piece and Kylie lowered the violin. Ramiro looked over his shoulder, a twinkle in his eye. She blushed a little.

"How is it that you play so incredibly well?" she asked, recalling that he worked on a cruise ship.

"I am a classical and jazz pianist. It's what I do—Entertain." His eyes danced. "Did you think I was a waiter?"

She laughed playfully. "Maybe. So tell me then, what's it like?"

He pivoted around on the seat, facing her comfortably, his every mannerism smooth and confident. "I play in a ten-piece show band, usually as the backup for guest entertainers. We do production shows as well—with a whole cast of singers and dancers. Jazz sets, the Top 40. It's all very exciting and high society, I assure you." A wink. "And when we dock, well . . . I visit my cousin." He laughed. "I'm living the dream, as they say!"

An inner pang. What must it be like to play in an orchestra, travelling to and from exotic places, meeting new and fascinating people? What a perpetual feast it must be. Mya and Keira came to mind then. Being a travelling musician wasn't a possibility for her, delightful as she imagined it to be.

"I can only dream of playing in an orchestra one day," she said, musing.

"Why only dream? You're very gifted." His gaze was intense, almost intimate.

She smiled wryly but didn't bother to explain. What did he care about her children, or family life? "One more song?" she asked.

He grinned, swivelling, and began to play Haydn's Serenade.

After that, he bid her adieu at the front doors without saying when he might return, although he did allude to being on a temporary hiatus—which she assumed meant he'd be around again before leaving the Island for another cruise.

He strolled away, leather satchel over his shoulder. And once again, that feeling of sunshine disappearing behind clouds.

"Pearl has requested tea time in the garden," Connie explained with a smile, having entered the library where Kylie and the girls were reclining. "A change of scenery, she said. Being that it's such a lovely day and all." She pushed a cart of tea things through the room and stopped at the

French doors.

"Oh, is she feeling better then?" Kylie asked, lowering her book.

"I should think so. Usually she skips tea if she's not up to it."

"Okay, girls, you heard Connie. Let's go!" She smiled cheerfully at her daughters, knowing they'd be pleased to have a snack. After collecting their shoes, they followed Connie over the terrace and down the walkway that led around the side of the house. Reaching the garden, they passed through the stone moongate and found Pearl already there waiting.

She wore a striped summer dress, hair neatly combed, and was sitting on a long cushioned couch. Jasmine, hibiscus, frangipani, and rose bushes surrounded the sitting area. The girls climbed up beside Pearl, their feet not quite reaching the ground. She said hello with a smile but stared out toward the sea with an absent look while Connie arranged the tray of refreshments. Kylie sat in an armchair across from them beside a banana tree.

"How are you feeling, Pearl," she asked, "any better?"

"I am much better, thank you." A brittle smile. The concealer beneath her eyes hadn't fully diffused the bags and a greyish tint showed through. "I overheard you and Ramiro playing this afternoon," she went on, "and I must say that it was really quite extraordinary."

"Oh thank you. I had no idea he was a professional—and on a cruise ship, no less! What an exciting life he must lead."

Pearl's expression darkened, eyes narrowing. "Yes. He is indeed very talented."

Kylie looked at her tea cup, considering. "I'm surprised you've never mentioned him before," she said, waiting a moment before making eye contact. "I mean, in years past."

They stared at one another.

"It is uncomfortable for me to say this in front of your daughters, Kylie, but I feel I must remind you of what we discussed in the library the day you first arrived. As I expressed, I do not wish for your father to know about my"—she lowered her voice—"current illness." She cast a downward glance at Mya and Keira beside her but they were too busy eating and chattering with each other to pay her any mind.

A tiny bird flitted by.

"Has Dad ever met him?"

Pearl seemed startled by the question, almost frightened, but as she opened her mouth to respond, Mya spilled her cup of orange juice beside her on the couch. Mya squealed and jumped up.

Pearl grabbed a folded cloth napkin from the table and blotted up the juice almost frantically. "It is alright, Mya, it is alright—do not fret!" Her eyes were wide, lines forming in her brow, hands trembling as she reached for another napkin. She seemed spooked.

Kylie stood as well, setting her China cup and saucer on the table. Mya had juice on her shorts and legs and needed to change. "I'll let Connie know about the spill," she said, gathering her daughters and leading them through the moongate.

Her last glimpse of Pearl was of her collapsing onto the couch, a yellowed cloth hanging in her hand, chin against her chest as she drooped forward. She looked defeated in some way.

Had the spilled juice really frazzled her so much—or was it Kylie's hint that Ramiro was a secret?

CHAPTER 11

The next morning, Kylie awoke to the muffled sounds of vomiting again, but she stayed in bed; knowing it was Pearl and not her children. She hoped it wasn't the flu.

After breakfast the girls wanted to swim, so Kylie spent the morning sunbathing and reading while watching over them. They ate lunch outside as well, then took a transit bus into town to buy groceries for dinner. With Pearl sick and Edward not due home until the next morning, Kylie decided to cook supper herself. She hadn't seen Trey since the day before and wondered if he'd spent the night at Cassidy's.

When she arrived back at the estate mid-afternoon and helped the girls down off the bus—a grocery bag in each of her hands—the sound of an approaching motor caused her to stop and look back.

A male rider on a scooter came whipping around the corner and pulled into the driveway. The helmet visor obscured his face but a leather satchel hung from his right shoulder to his left side.

Her heartbeat quickened.

Ramiro.

He cut the engine and put his feet down, pulling the helmet off as he did. "Ladies," he said with a nod and a smile. "My timing is perfect, I see." The gate finished closing behind them as he stepped off the bike and hung the helmet from the handle bar, a whiff of gasoline in the air. He took the grocery bags from Kylie as though it were the most natural thing to do, and they walked up the poinciana-lined driveway together.

Keira knocked on the door when they reached the house and they all stood on the portico waiting.

Kylie turned to look at Ramiro. "Pearl is expecting you? She's been sick all day."

"Yes. Yes, I'm aware." He looked away and she watched the side of his face until the front door opened and Connie beckoned them in.

While Ramiro went to see Pearl, Kylie began unpacking the groceries, trying not to guess at the interaction going on upstairs. It made little sense.

Descending steps sounded only moments later.

"It's such a gorgeous day, would you care for a walk, by chance?" he asked breathlessly, entering the kitchen as she put the final item in the fridge.

She looked at him too quickly to hide her surprise.

"The railway trail," he explained, smiling, "and bring the girls too, if you like. Or do you have other plans?"

Her heart thudded in her chest, confusion growing. What were his intentions? He gazed at her like a man in pursuit. Did he usually visit Pearl this often or was it becoming a pretense to see Kylie? She'd sensed a mutual attraction from day one, and it seemed stronger each time they met.

She glanced at the clock above the kitchen dresser to note the time. "You know, a walk does sound nice," she said smiling, heart pounding. Was she actually saying yes? "But we'd need to be back by four, for tea."

He laughed. "Yes, certainly. We must not snub tradition." A wink.

She hesitated. After an active day outdoors, the children were looking forward to relaxing—they'd be disappointed and inclined to grumble—but if they stayed behind with the housekeeper,

Kylie would be completely alone with Ramiro . . .

A heady sensation came over her.

"I'll see if Connie wouldn't mind watching the girls." Though her Christian faith was sounding the alarm bells, she tuned it out. She wasn't a child in need of a chaperone. And besides, it was a public walkway.

That arranged, Kylie went upstairs to freshen up while Ramiro went outside to wait. She checked her makeup and scrunched her curls, debating whether or not to change from her long-flowing summer dress into something more practical, but decided against it. Though reluctant to admit it to herself, she wanted to look as good as possible.

After scowling at her appearance in the mirror, she left the room.

This wasn't a date.

Ramiro stood in the shade beneath the palmetto, texting on his smartphone. He looked up at the sound of the door shutting, and grinned, slipping the phone in his pant pocket and closing the gap between them.

A short stroll down the sunbaked main road brought them to one of numerous entry points to the Bermuda Railway Trail: eighteen miles of abandoned rail bed maneuvering its way along the rocky coastline and lush terrain of the island.

They walked side by side while enjoying the scenery, shoulders nearly touching, speaking only occasionally. Sunshine warmed her skin, making it tingle, a breeze kissing her collarbones and sliding through her hair. They paused at a vista between mangroves to take in the ocean view. Turquoise water spanned out before them, dark patches of coral here and there, and sailboats in the distance.

Ramiro stood slightly behind her, silent. Acutely aware of his energy and close proximity, an ache formed in her throat, eyes watering. If he were Drew, she would have leaned back against his chest while his arms enfolded her. Instead her spine went rigid and she blinked a few times to clear her vision.

But the panorama soon liquefied again and she looked down at the ground, focusing on a piece of driftwood amongst the shrubbery.

Ramiro made a remark about the view, his mellow voice so close to her ear that goosebumps rose on her skin. Though he didn't move she began to imagine the touch of his fingertips on her arm, slipping down and taking her hand. Pictured him turning her around, toward him. The sun above him, behind him; bleaching the top of his hair while darkening the sides. Smoldering mocha eyes looked down at her, a tiny mole on the left side of his upper lip. She envisioned her hand reaching up to touch his cheek. Felt the stubble beneath. He smiled into her palm, face changing.

Drew.

The image vanished, the piece of driftwood at her feet filling her focus once again.

A brown skink lizard climbed up out of the grass and scooted across the bark, pausing on the surface to stare at her.

She turned away and smiled at Ramiro, feeling reserved. "Shall we head back?"

His face was neutral, unreadable.

"I suppose we must," he said. A half smile.

They resumed walking the trail and he talked about his passion for music, sharing anecdotes from his experiences on the cruise ship. It was an inexhaustible subject for her and she was soon sharing stories of her own, relaxing. But the jaunt back to the house went by too quickly and a pang tightened in her chest as they reached the entrance gate to her father's estate. She entered the passcode and the gates opened.

Ramiro went to his scooter, lifting the helmet. She didn't want him to leave; but put on a casual smile to mask the feeling.

"Till next time," he said pleasantly, swinging his leg over the scooter and driving off with a wave.

She wandered up the hill between the scarlet trees, tumbling petals tickling her sandaled feet as she walked. The sky above the estate was overcast with passing clouds; a long lonely evening stretching out before her.

Inside, Connie had already set out tea and refreshments in the library and had served the children, who were finishing up. No one else was present, and since it was already twenty past four, not likely to be either.

"Would you like a tea, miss?" she asked, looking up as Kylie entered the room.

"Thank you, no. Normally I would but I'm parched. I'll grab myself a glass of water—no, no, don't trouble yourself, I'll be going to the kitchen in a moment anyway. Is Pearl joining us?"

"I think not. She came down after you left and asked about Ramiro. Said his scooter was still in the driveway and wanted to know where he was." A pointed look.

Heat climbed her cheeks.

"So, I told her he'd gone for a walk on the railway trail." Connie pushed the tea cart toward the door as she talked. She stopped when she reached Kylie's side, dropping her voice to a confidential tone. "She asked me if you'd gone along with him. I'm sorry, but I couldn't lie."

"It's not a secret, Connie." Hiding her irritation, she called out to her daughters: "Girls, will you join me in the kitchen while I make supper?" She met Connie's eyes again and forced a smile. "Thanks again for watching Mya and Keira, I appreciate it." Understanding the conversation was over, the housekeeper gave a nod and pushed the cart out of the room.

Entering the kitchen, Kylie discovered Pearl sitting there at the table. She wore yoga pants and a sports bra, with a crisp towel draped over her shoulders. A near empty bottle of water sat in front of her and sweat glistened at her hair line. She stood up to greet them, welcoming the children to have a seat. Kylie felt a knot of jealousy in her stomach as Pearl rooted through a drawer in the kitchen dresser: she was perfectly sculpted from head to toe, like a professional athlete.

She withdrew two coloring books and a box of crayons, setting them down for the girls. "Kylie, may I speak with you privately in the sitting room?" she asked, heading for the hallway.

With no chance to refuse, Kylie trailed after her and sat down on the gestured-at settee while Pearl remained standing. Her hands were on her hips; a distinct aura of interrogation about it all.

"Your father will be home tomorrow," she said, "and I have not been well, as you know."

Kylie clasped her hands together in her lap, knees together, back stiff. She felt like a child who'd be up to mischief and was about to get a scolding. Where was this going?

"You are also aware that my cousin does not come here while Edward is at home."

Nausea filled her throat, pulse quickening.

Pearl dropped her hands to her sides. "If Ramiro continues to seek out *your* company whenever he visits me, Ed—your father—will soon find out. He will learn of it either from a slip of your tongue, or from one of the children's."

"Can I ask why you don't want Dad to know?" Her hands felt cold.

"I have already told you. I do not want him worrying about me. I will be recovered soon enough and so there is no need to trouble him." A note of impatience sounded in the last bit.

"But can't he know about your cousin without having to know about your illness?"

Pearl looked away.

"Is Ramiro really your cousin?" She had to know; for her father's sake . . .

"What exactly are you implying?" Pearl faced her directly again, chestnut eyes luminous with a look of surprise. Or was it fear?

Kylie flushed, back-paddled. "Nothing. I'm sorry."

Pearl reached for her temples, hands trembling, and closed her eyes for a moment. "My headache is returning. I must retire early." She began to leave the room. "Good-night."

Kylie watched her walk away.

Despite being visibly shaken, Pearl hadn't actually denied the allegation.

So if Ramiro wasn't her cousin . . . who was he?

CHAPTER 12

Saturday morning, Kylie again awoke to the muffled sounds of vomiting.

Sunlight streamed into the room, glinting off the mirror above the dresser; the rhythm of the rolling sea in the distance. It was just after seven.

She turned over and faced the bedroom door, listening as the sounds of retching ceased. Though she'd seen Pearl looking pale and shaky in the afternoon and evenings, the vomiting seemed to be limited to the early morning. The flu would have her barfing any time of day, and she never drank excessively or showed signs of alcoholism. So, perhaps the illness was indeed serious—like cancer—and Pearl was lying about the severity. But the idea that Ramiro was visiting to "help" now seemed about as far-fetched as him being a relative.

She had to talk to her father about it. He'd be home late morning or early afternoon, she wasn't sure which, and his arrival couldn't come soon enough. Keeping quiet was no longer an option. A particular thought had troubled her during the night: If Ramiro was actually Pearl's lover, the vomiting might be morning sickness.

Edward arrived home mid-afternoon. "Hello, hello," he called out from the front entrance as Kylie and the girls left the dining room and went to meet him. He stood beaming at them, shopping bags in each hand. "Presents for everyone!"

He slipped off his shoes and asked them to join him in the sitting room.

"Dad, you really didn't have to buy all these gifts."

He waved her off. "Nonsense, of course I did. How often do I get to spoil my granddaughters?"

Mya and Keira sat down on the chaise lounge, eagerly opening their parcels as he passed them over.

Kylie offered him a drink but he declined, patting his belly with both hands and explaining that he'd just finished a late lunch in town. He sat down on the settee next to the children and stretched out his arms, adjusting his glinting wristwatch and letting out a breathy exhale. "Well, Mya, Keira, how do you like 'em?" A nod toward the opened gifts.

Both girls marvelled over the items, talking over one another, thanking him and giggling as he asked engaging questions; indulging their childish sense of humor. Kylie sat down on a Chippendale armchair and crossed one leg over the other, enjoying the banter and occasionally joining in, though thinking about Pearl all the while. The woman was right—sooner or later the children would mention Ramiro innocently, and in passing. It would be far better to have talked to her father about it before that happened, even though Pearl wished for her to keep quiet. But it wasn't going to be an easy topic to broach. The last thing she wanted to do was facilitate a potential fallout between her father and his girlfriend when she'd only been here one week and wanted to stay four more.

"So, how's the ol' stepdad?" he asked, halting her ruminations.

Every few months this question came up and year after year she gave the same dutiful answer in one form or another: "Dean is fine, same as usual. Treats Mom well."

"Good." He nodded and seemed satisfied. "She deserves that. I couldn't sleep at night if ever I thought she might be unhappy."

Did he still miss her after all these years? The choice to divorce hadn't been mutual; his consent capitulated. "Workaholic" her mother had called him, saying she'd "languished" with loneliness in that marriage. Incidentally, a career transfer offer to Canada so enticed her that she chose to abandon husband and son, and start over—with a new life and not long after, a new husband. Yet despite the loss of his wife and daughter, Edward hadn't changed his working habits in the slightest. Instead, he plunged into his work with what seemed a renewed vigor.

Kylie glanced out into the hallway. Pearl hadn't joined them for breakfast and later requested lunch be brought up to her room. Though she didn't appear to be nearby, Kylie lowered her voice just in case.

"Dad, I need to talk to you about something private, as soon as you have the chance."

"Is everything alright?"

"I just can't discuss it in front of the girls, is all."

"Right, let's get the girls set up with an activity then—"

Pearl entered the room without a sound, her shadow in both their peripheries, and he stopped speaking abruptly.

They turned toward her.

Dainty slippers had muffled her footfall: Either she came down the stairs in a flash or was already descending when Kylie lowered her voice.

"Darling—" Edward hefted himself up and went to Pearl, gathering her into an embrace and kissing her. Though she returned the kiss, she extricated herself and held him at arm's length, her smile slight. She made no eye contact with Kylie.

Only then did Edward notice her dressing gown. "Are you unwell today?"

She let go of his arms and stepped back, her every movement and posture graceful and fine, perhaps even calculated. She was not one to make fast or jerky movements. "I am alright, my love. I simply took advantage of a Saturday morning and slept in. I lunched in my room as well. When I happened to hear your voice and knew you had arrived home, I couldn't wait to greet you. Now that I have done so, I'll go back upstairs and get dressed, if you will excuse me." This latter bit she seemed to address to Kylie and the children.

With a sweet smile and droop of her eyelashes, she left the room.

"I guess we'll have to talk later, Kylie," Edward said with evident distraction, heading for the hallway and presumably the staircase to follow Pearl. "I'll be back in a little while." He winked and she faked a smile.

They didn't return until tea time; Pearl immaculately dressed and hair coiffed. Edward was in great spirits, announcing he was taking them all out for dinner. "Where is my son, by the way?" He glanced around the library with a jerk as though he'd just noticed Trey's absence.

"I believe he's out with Cassidy," Connie replied, refilling his tea cup and offering him another serving of pastries, which he accepted.

"Cassidy? Oh, right, yes, Cassidy. The girl. When will he be home?"

"I couldn't say, sir. He never tells."

"He'll have to fend for himself then if he doesn't come home till after we've left. I won't be waiting around." Anger tinged his voice, unusual for his genial personality. There seemed to be some hard feelings between the two of them. Had there been a falling out at some point or was it the natural pain of separation that occurs when a young man strives for independence? Trey was twenty-three after all, and still living at home.

Later that evening, after returning from a lovely fine-dining experience in which Pearl had made a remarkable effort to be conversational and engaged, they all climbed out of Edward's KIA Picanto and were heading for the house when a taxi pulled up outside the gates.

Trey and Cassidy emerged.

Edward stopped walking and stared at them long and hard before turning to go indoors with Pearl.

The young couple trudged up the driveway hand in hand, Trey looking at the ground and Cassidy giving a friendly wave at Kylie, who waved back.

Not feeling the need to wait however, Kylie took her girls indoors and helped get them ready for bed. They chattered away, giddy after a fun night with Grandpa, and it was hard for her to concentrate on their specific words—she was too distracted—but she made an effort to interact cheerfully nonetheless. Though she'd had a wonderful evening with her father at the restaurant, there was no chance to talk to him alone about Ramiro, and her anxiety had now reached the point of nervous tension. Pearl's unusual effort to engage with everyone seemed suspect too, like overcompensation. A guilty conscience maybe?

With Mya and Keira settled in their beds, Kylie went in search of her father, hoping he'd be alone—but her heart sank when she found him in the library. Trey and Cassidy were lounging together on one of the sofas close to where he'd pulled up a wing chair; and he was already in the process of dealing out playing cards on the table between them.

Her father looked up, grinning with evident pleasure and saying she was just in time to join them.

She feigned interest and took a seat on the sofa adjacent her brother and his girlfriend.

Whatever trace of anger her father had felt toward Trey earlier in the evening seemed gone at present, though perhaps he was good at hiding it. That, or Cassidy's infectious laughter had mellowed him. She was certainly having that effect on Kylie.

The French doors stood open to let in fresh air; the rolling of the sea blending with reggae music on the stereo. Lamps lit the room with cozy lighting.

"Did Pearl go to bed?" Kylie asked.

Edward nodded and reached for his cigar box, offering one to Trey, who accepted. "You know how she is."

Only she didn't know.

Had Pearl always retired early or was it a new trait?

They finished the first round and Edward offered everyone drinks from the sideboard. The others opted for Dark 'N Stormies—ginger beer and rum—while Kylie declined, detesting the overt spiciness of it. She asked for a Swizzle instead—orange juice and rum. They started in on a second round and she found herself stealing glances at her brother; pleased to see him relaxing. His normal brooding demeanour had lifted and he looked younger, almost childish, glancing at his dad side-long, eyes lighting with every shared laugh. A flush mantled his cheeks . . . from the drink?

"Do you guys play cards often?" she asked, imagining them doing this on a regular basis and feeling a twinge of envy.

Trey looked away, face darkening.

"This would be the first time in months," Edward said, taking a pull from his cigar. "I came in here to sulk, truth be told, and found these two hogging the TV." He laughed and gestured at Cassidy. "But this dear girl suggested we play cards instead."

"Why sulky?"

He waved her off. "Oh, Pearl and all that. I was right annoyed when after such a perfect night together she decides to go and cut it short. So typical." He took another pull from his cigar. "Said she wasn't feeling well,"—exhaled—"her go-to excuse these days."

Trey set down his cards and folded his arms over his chest. The sullen look was back.

As much as she wanted to probe for more

information about Pearl, she decided to drop the subject for her brother's sake; hoping his spirited look would soon return. Once he and Cassidy left for the night, she'd bring it up again.

They played a few more rounds and had a couple more drinks, her pulse quickening whenever she thought about what she had to tell her father, then slowing again as she tempered herself. Eventually she got up to shut the French doors, feeling chilly. Cassidy carried most of the conversation for everyone, keeping them all jovial, but now tiredness was getting the best of even her. Though Trey seemed to brighten again when they ceased to discuss Pearl, he gradually withdrew as Edward withdrew. Midnight came and the cards were put away. The young couple said their good-nights; Cassidy snuggling up against Trey's shoulder as they left the room.

"You don't mind her spending the night?" Kylie asked.

Edward blinked at his daughter, straining to focus. He must have been deep in thought, or perhaps only dozing. "Oh sheesh, I don't care, he's an adult." He rubbed his eyes with his thumb and index. "Usually he's the one who doesn't come home at night . . . I rarely see the girl here. Can't even remember her name half the time." He made moves to heave himself up out of his seat.

"Dad, wait—there's something I need to talk to you about first."

He sat back down.

Heart pounding, she clasped her hands together in her lap to keep from fidgeting, and drew in a deep breath. "Do you know about Pearl's cousin? His name is Ramiro. . . . He visits every couple of days."

A long silence followed and she held his gaze, searching his eyes for understanding as he sat still and unmoving, processing. She soon found it.

"I'm sure that you already know full well that I don't," he said finally. "Go on then, tell me what he looks like."

She described him as best as she could.

"And what does he do while he's here?"

There wasn't much to tell and truth was, she didn't know what he and Pearl did in private. She described what she'd seen each time but made no verbal assumptions; he could come to his own conclusions. She was also careful to leave out her own interactions with Ramiro, not wanting to complicate the matter. It would be mortifying to admit anyway; how could she possibly explain herself?

At some point Edward's shoulders had slumped, though she only noticed it now.

"She swore you to secrecy, I presume?"

"In a manner of speaking. I'm so sorry, Dad, I wasn't sure what to do."

He stared at his knees. A breathy exhale. "Well, such is life. I'm going to head to bed now, Kylie. I know you're troubled about it and it's a shame you got stuck in such an embarrassing situation—but truth be told, darling, all said and done, I'd really rather not have known." He pushed himself up. "Don't worry yourself about it any longer, I'll be fine. Mum's the word."

He left the room.

She stared at the doorway and shadowed hallway beyond it for a long time, gripping the arm of the couch with her fingertips. Though it was a relief to have finally told her father what was going on in the house, there were still no answers. And her own interactions with Ramiro added a personal level of discomfort and fear. What was she getting mixed up in? She considered praying about it but already knew that she should avoid Ramiro henceforward. Being separated from her husband was distressing enough, why risk a guilty conscience as well? Yes—she must keep far away from Ramiro.

With this reluctant resolve the mundanity of life seemed to press in all around. There was a feeling of let down, of disappointment, of dullness. Her throat ached as though she'd been weeping yet her eyes remained dry.

Because even though she was still married and Ramiro could possibly be Pearl's paramour, Kylie hungered to see him again.

CHAPTER 13

Andrew Cadore leaned back in his seat and stared out the oval window overlooking the wing of the plane and the Atlantic ocean. It was Sunday afternoon. Through the gaps in the clouds, Bermuda came into view: that uniquely fish-shaped Island surrounded by coral reefs.

After much prayer and deliberation he'd made arrangements with the golf club to take a vacation week. But he'd decided not to inform Kylie of his plans until he got there. Half the summer was too long to go without seeing his daughters and he wanted to share some of their experiences in Bermuda. He doubted Kylie would want to see him though, much less spend time with him, but he figured they could just take turns spending time with the children—and he would stay at a hotel, not Edward's.

Up until now he'd been patient, giving her space—but he needed to be more proactive now, before it was too late. His marriage was sinking like a ship and he wasn't going to just drown without any attempts to reach the surface. He was losing everything he cherished most, maybe even already had, and felt instinctively in his spirit that he must go to her.

Later that afternoon, after finishing at the airport, he checked into a hotel in Hamilton and decided to decompress after a full day of travel. He'd wait until Monday to contact Kylie—with resumed energy.

The sunny balcony in his fourth floor room beckoned with a glimmering view of the ocean. This is where they'd first met and fallen in love. Maybe it was also where they could start over, where they could find each other again. He could only hope.

Kylie spent much of Sunday afternoon on a reclining beach chair under a palm tree while Mya and Keira swam and ran about.

Pearl joined everyone at breakfast time for a change, well-dressed and bright-eyed; startling Kylie with an invite for her and the girls to join her and Edward for church service that morning.

Edward wasn't one to attend church apart from Christmas and Easter, but the greatest surprise was Pearl.

"I didn't know you went to church," Kylie said in response, trying not to look shocked.

"It's a new thing," her father explained before Pearl could say a word. "Blame Connie." A laugh. "She's made an Anglican convert of Pearl."

"And you too?"

He winked, acting like his usual self, as though she hadn't told him the night before that his girlfriend might have a secret lover. "I play more of the role of chauffeur," he said. "I'm in it for lunch at the bistro afterwards." He rubbed his belly. "I've got to make it worth my while, you see—isn't that right, my dear?" A glance at Pearl.

Pearl was bent over her plate, picking at her food, chignoned hair exquisite with rosette curls. She looked up and gave Edward a soft, somewhat absentminded smile. Kylie wondered vaguely how long her updo took to arrange, how many pins, and how much hairspray. A work of art, nonetheless.

After breakfast, they drove to Hamilton together and parked beneath a row of palm trees beside the church: a Gothic Revival style cathedral. The service was indeed lovely and traditional, but Kylie couldn't recall much of the sermon afterward and knew she'd been daydreaming. Pearl's attention, on the other hand, seemed riveted throughout, while Edward held a consistently glazed look. During lunch, however, Pearl's energy became evanescent and by the time they reached home, she was the picture of exhaustion, yawning every few minutes. She went straight upstairs for a nap. Edward, not even hiding his anger and annoyance, collected his golf clubs and drove away, leaving Kylie and the girls to their lonesome.

Eventually Mya and Keira had tired of swimming and Kylie left the shade to spend time building sandcastles with them.

They'd been working a good half hour together when the French doors off the library opened and Trey and Cassidy stepped out onto the terrace; a platter of drinks in Cassidy's hands. They both wore swimsuits and sunglasses.

"You-hoo, I've got cocktails," Cassidy sang, taking careful steps down the lawn and beaming with a genuine smile. She set the tray down on a table by the beach chairs. "My goodness, what beautiful castles you've made, girls! Kylie—you're glistening—go sit down in the shade and I'll hand you a drink. I've got juiceboxes for the kiddos too."

Trey nodded a greeting at his sister, shed his glasses, and went straight for the water.

Cassidy served the drinks and the four of them lounged for a while, watching Trey swim. The girls, unable to sit still for long, were soon inspired to swim again, and Kylie helped Keira don her life jacket.

"I'll swim later," Cassidy said, stretching out on her chair and crossing her feet at the ankles, toes sparkling with purple nail polish. "First I'ma work on my tan. I just love tanning here, you know, it's so private. But go to the public beach and it's string-bikini-city. Bleh, no thank you."

"Do you guys go to the public beach often?"

"No, almost never—I hate it. We swim here instead when we can. It's nice not having that pressure."

"Pressure?"

"Yeah—of always wondering who he may or may not be checking out."

"Is he like that?"

"Like what?"

"The kind of guy who stares at other girls in front of his girlfriend."

Cassidy lowered her sunglasses and looked over the rims to make eye contact. "No, of course not, but you know what I mean. They're sly about it." She replaced her sunglasses. "The point is I don't know which girls he's looking at—I can only guess. Plus, it's mortifying to be seen in a swimsuit. I don't like being judged." She pointed at the rolls between her two-piece. A belly-button ring glinted in the middle.

"You're a lovely girl, Cassidy, you've got nothing to worry about." Ouch. Lies. There was plenty to worry about, no matter what a woman's size.

"I know, I know—'fat is beautiful, love yourself'—but I could repeat that mantra a thousand times a day and still never believe it."

"Why not?"

"Well, do you believe it?"

Kylie's cheeks burned. She'd backed herself into a corner.

"You're hesitating—that says everything." A musical laugh. "Oh don't feel bad, you were only trying to be nice."

"No, you're getting the wrong idea, Cassidy, that's not at all what I meant!" She glanced down at her slender frame and sighed. There was no way out but to be honest. "Let me explain. My husband, he . . . okay, the thing is, I used to feel quite attractive, actually thought I was one of the better looking ones. I wasn't intimidated by other women." Her heart drummed in her chest. Cassidy lowered her sunglasses again. "But then I found out that he was—" She exhaled. "He was using porn. Now I can't even look at myself in the mirror for more than a few seconds at a time. All I see are the flaws. Just like that,"—she snapped her fingers—"all my confidence evaporated."

"Are you flipping kidding me?" Cassidy said, censoring herself in front of the children. "Look at you! I'd give anything to look like you."

"But that's exactly my point. I'm slim, yeah, but it made no difference." A pause. "I truly meant it when I said you're lovely. You have a knack for setting people at ease, a sparkle in your eyes, and such a contagious laugh. I admire that."

"Yeah, well." A bashful smile. "Oh by the way, you might as well know—Trey watches porn too. Isn't it normal?"

"What, he told you?"

"Uh yeah,"—a laugh—"we watch it together in fact. You look shocked, don't be. I'd rather watch it with him and know what he's see-ing, than have him feel like he has to sneak behind my back. No offense though, I don't mean anything about you of course—I just mean that I'd rather he not have to lie to me about it." She shrugged a shoulder. "I figure if he gets to enjoy it I might as well enjoy it too."

Kylie's breathing shallowed. She put her hand to her collarbone and rested it there. It was cold against her skin, despite the glaring sun.

"Do you though?"

"Enjoy it? Yeah, if the guys are hot. And as long as nothing too weird goes on."

"No, but really. Would you watch it on your own?"

Another laugh. "I don't know. Maybe! I didn't before Trey but I was pretty green in those days."

Kylie reached for her drink and took a sip to steady herself.

"Cassidy, I know this is really personal," she said after a moment, "but . . . why do you feel so uncomfortable at the beach when you don't mind Trey watching porn? I'm just trying to understand."

"Easy. Because the girls at the beach are real. Porn isn't real—it's just a fantasy."

"But the actresses are real."

"Not really. They've had surgery and things, and there's lighting effects and stuff. And anyway, he can't touch them. I don't have to worry he's gonna cheat on me if it's not a real person."

Kylie nodded, excusing herself to go and ask Mya and Keira to stay closer to the shore, welcoming the distraction. The growing tension in her temples threatened a headache.

When she returned to the chairs, Cassidy had stood up and was applying sunscreen.

"I'll join you, if you're going to swim," Kylie said, not wanting to continue the conversation any longer. She might say something about Trey she'd end up regretting: it was hard enough not to scream, let alone speak calmly.

After swimming, they towelled off and went indoors to dress.

Keira needed a bandage for a scuff on her elbow, so Kylie rifled through her dresser drawers in search of the box of Band-Aids she'd seen the first day they arrived; but came up short. They were gone. Odd. Had someone come into her room and taken them? If so, when. And was it really the only box in the entire house? With a shrug, she looked through the drawers in the ensuite bathroom and found several boxes there.

They missed tea time, since Connie was off on Sundays and not there to remind them, and Edward hadn't returned from golfing yet either. It seemed likely he'd decided to dine at the club. Pearl passed by them in the hallway downstairs, evidently on her way to the workout room, but she didn't stop to talk to anyone.

On a whim, Kylie begged Trey to prepare supper for them, eager to try more of his delectable cooking. Her anger toward him earlier had faded a little but still simmered on low. She hoped playing the violin after dinner would soothe away the rest. Cassidy was keen on the idea of Trey cooking too and they soon had him convinced.

After assessing the contents of the freezer

and cupboards, he decided to make Portuguese red bean soup—a hearty ham dish. To Kylie's surprise, he even let Mya and Keira help with the preparations. The girls were thrilled of course and by the time dinner was served, they both beamed proudly over their accomplishments. Trey seemed to take pleasure in giving them the credit, even cracking a smile or two at times, a light in his eyes. Whenever he was in a room with Edward he seemed childish, even shy, but standing there beside his nieces, actually engaging with them, he looked more grown up than Kylie had ever seen him before.

As dinner was now ready to serve, Kylie went to the workout room in search of Pearl, and found it empty. She then went upstairs, thinking about Trey as she knocked on the bedroom door. Though their mother did all the cooking when they were kids, there were a few times in childhood when Trey had specifically asked to help their father with gardening or yard work and had been denied. Edward was fastidious when it came to such things and preferred to work on his own, though these days he paid a gardener to do the work.

Receiving a mumbled decline from Pearl, Kylie returned to the dining room and joined the others.

After supper and a group effort to clear away the dishes, Trey prepared a caramel flan for dessert; a recipe Cassidy had given him. The rest of them went to the library to watch TV while waiting for it to be ready. The kids commandeered the remote—begging for cartoons. Cassidy suggested leaving the main seating area to chat privately away from the children, and Kylie followed her to a sitting nook in the corner of the room next to Edward's computer desk.

"You have a good poker face, but are you pissed with Trey?" Cassidy asked without warning, sideswiping her bangs and leaning back in the arm-chair. She wore a long T-shirt over her leggings and it was the first time Kylie had seen her without fake eyelashes. She must have removed them after swimming. Her brown eyes seemed brighter without them, fuller.

Heat crept up the back of Kylie's neck and she blinked. "I think disappointed is a better word. But it's really none of my business." Goosebumps rose on her skin despite it being a warm night.

Cassidy looked troubled. "Is this the reason you and your husband split, if you don't mind me asking? Trey says you're separated, but he doesn't know why."

"Yes—that was the main reason."

"And he just left without a fight?"

"In a manner of speaking, but he's no wuss. He's always been a gentleman that way, doesn't push. He just knows that when I've made up my mind, I've made up my mind. I can be pretty stubborn." A half smile. "But I honestly don't think he'd have left so easily if he'd known it was going to last this long. . . . I didn't deceive him though, I was just taking it one day at a time."

"Change your mind after he left?"

"More like . . . it's just that, I found with each week that passed by—though I missed him and wanted him back—badly—I couldn't see acting like nothing had changed between us. Does that make sense? Pretending everything was normal. . . . Because I always envisioned the same result. Which was some sort of a faux relationship in which I'd be paranoid to leave him home by himself, never able to trust his word again."

No response. Cassidy stared across the room at a wall of bookshelves, looking pensive.

Why share this with her brother's girlfriend of all people, whom she barely knew? Her own mother had made little attempt to understand. And though her closest friends seemed to get it, none of them had experienced it themselves.

Cassidy had.

"I know you think letting him use it . . . openly . . . would have prevented this," Kylie continued, keeping her voice low so the kids wouldn't overhear. "And I understand what you mean by that. But isn't it a bit like saying 'it's okay if he goes to strip clubs, as long as he has my permission'?"

Cassidy frowned.

"Does he go to strip clubs?"

"Of course not! Though I guess it's not much different." A shrug.

"But it's not even that really," Kylie went on, shaking her head. "See the one thing I can't seem to get over, more than anything else . . . is the thought of making love while he's—"

"—picturing someone else."

"Yes!"

Cassidy's voice was flat now. "Because he's not really making love to you, is he, he's just f— sorry, he's just doing the chick du *jour* in his mind."

A nod.

They fell into a solemn silence then broken only by the drifting laughter and cartoon voices from the TV.

Yes. A warm body rather than a cherished lover. It was like having a third person in the bedroom, or a dozen others for that matter, which only he was seeing. And her? Eclipsed, invisible.

"I do get pissed at him sometimes," Cassidy said. "Your brother. Like I wish it was just the two of us again, you know, like the first few weeks? You look embarrassed, I'm sorry. Is it TMI? Alright, so anyway, after about a month-ish? he asked if I'd watch a 'film' with him, just to try it. I figured alright, why not, might be fun. But ever since that night he fumbles for his laptop or phone the moment we start kissing—doesn't even ask! Ticks me right off. That or we'll be hanging out and I'll be working on homework or texting, and suddenly realize he's already watching it—right across the room from me. Then when the video ends, he expects me to just drop everything and . . . " She rolled her eyes. "It's like I'm not enough, like I'm being used. Most of the time I just try to enjoy watching it with him instead of complaining, so it's a mutual benefit and all that, but I still miss that feeling of being his whole world."

Trey entered the room pushing a cart of dessert dishes.

Kylie forced a smile and what she hoped was a cheerful disposition. Her appetite was gone but he'd worked hard on preparing the flan and she didn't want to hurt him. Soon enough Mya and Keira would go to bed and she'd be free to play the violin. Until then there was nothing to do but push down the wave of grief threatening to overflow.

A hundred times she'd hovered over her smartphone, typing and deleting text after text, aching to her very core to have her husband back, missing him every single day. Every time he came to the house to see the children—their home—she had to avoid eye contact and keep her distance, knowing that with one open look into his eyes she might throw herself on his neck and never let go.

Because even though he'd been to months of counselling, it didn't undo what had happened nor did it guarantee it wouldn't happen again. And couple's counselling? No thank you. She had unknowingly been his whore for an entire year. If she took him back, she might have to spend the rest her life living that way.

After reading bedtime stories and settling Mya and Keira to bed, Kylie went to the music room and played for an hour, but the music didn't have its usual lulling effect. Perhaps talking to Cassidy had brought the pain too close to the surface; closer than she was used to.

Letting out a breathy exhale, she returned the violin to its stand and sat very still, hands in her lap, willing herself to calm. If she moved, she might begin weeping.

A clock ticked on the wall.

In time, she heard her father return home and go upstairs, followed by the muffled sounds of an argument between him and Pearl. Eventually that died down and the house was silent again, apart from the clock and the murmur of rolling waves on the shore.

She relived a starry night when she and Drew had walked that same shoreline arm in arm. Both barefoot, tingling water engulfing their ankles before releasing to slide back across the sand. She wore a summer halter dress, grey cast in the moon-light, and he khaki shorts with a tee. His black hair, tousled, glimmered, just like his eyes when he smiled. His arm was warm, his whole side warm, and she leaned into him, nestling her cheek against his shoulder. They watched whitecaps dance across the distant waters. He stroked her hair and kissed her cheekbone, so tender. Her heart was full. Later they went inside . . . opened the bedroom windows to let in the melody of the waves . . . and made love under soft lamplight.

Gone.

All gone now.

She blinked and looked down at her lap. How long had she been sitting here trance-like? Tomorrow her father would return to work and she wondered if she'd see Ramiro Airoso again.

Her stomach did a flip flop at the thought.

Was she mad? The man was almost certainly Pearl's lover.

CHAPTER 14

Kylie spent most of Monday morning in a wing-back chair in the library, immersing herself in a romance novel she'd purchased at the grocery store. Self-torture basically, but at least it helped to pass the time. While she read, the children used the coffee table as a station to draw pictures and later to fill out postcards for Drew and their grandparents back in Ontario. Pearl joined them for lunch and when Kylie mentioned her plans to take the girls to the Perot Post Office afterwards, she invited herself to come along.

They took a transit bus and arrived at the whitewashed, black-shuttered historical building around two o'clock. It didn't take long to get stamps and finish their quest, and they were soon back outside on the sunny sidewalk, planning what to do next. Pearl announced that she hoped Kylie didn't mind but she'd sent a text to Ramiro arranging to meet with him briefly in Queen Elizabeth's Park—right behind the post office.

"I have been meaning to lend a certain book to him," she said, adjusting her droopy sunhat, "and decided to bring it along with me, since he lives nearby. He is anxious to read it."

Kylie's pulse thrummed with the unexpected announcement.

In the park, now?

She removed her sunglasses and discreetly checked her reflection in the lenses—hoping her shorts and tank top were flattering—while taking the children around the side of the building. There they followed Pearl through open iron gates leading into the park, and walked along a flagstone path through and around manicured lawns and flowerbeds. They soon reached a skinny cluster of palms encircled by a koi pond.

He was waiting for them in the shade of foliage, scrolling his phone.

Pearl called out his name with a cheery hello and he turned at the sound of her voice, slipping the phone into his pocket. His stern expression softened into a smile when he noticed Kylie and the children. He seemed surprised, taken aback; had he expected Pearl to be alone?

Pearl reached into her purse and pulled out an old paperback. "Darling, I have the book you wanted." She passed it to him, cover facing downward.

He hesitated before opening the flap on his his satchel and tucking it inside. Though his demeanor was casual, something flickered in his eyes as he held prolonged eye contact with Pearl. An unspoken word between them perhaps?

Pearl took a step backward then and lost her footing, catching her balance by grabbing the raised stone edge of the pond. She grimaced. "Clumsy me, it is these shoes." She lifted a foot to show her high-heeled fringe sandals. "Oh dear, it is bleeding a little," she said, putting a knuckle to her lips. "Ramiro, do you have a bandage in your bag?"

He rooted in his satchel and withdrew a blue and white box of Band-Aids. "Ms. Cadore," he said, while handing it to Pearl, "may I speak with you privately for a moment?"

Still bewildered by Pearl's unusual display of clumsiness, it took a moment for Kylie to realize what he'd asked—and she glanced over at the children without answering. They were leaning over the pond and exclaiming amongst themselves, discussing the various koi in the water.

"Pearl can watch them, yes?" he said, answering her tacit question. "It will only take a moment, I assure you."

Before she could respond, he tucked her arm in his and led her out of the foliage back to the main pathway where they soon approached a pergola, draped with flowering bougainvillea. She glanced over her shoulder as they walked; hoping no friends of her father were around who might recognize her.

Rather than entering the pergola, Ramiro veered off the path and led her to a spot on the grass next to a quaint lamppost. He released her arm and stood facing her, eyes intense. The top buttons of his shirt were undone, a pair of folded sunglasses hanging in the gap. She couldn't help noticing his waxed chest, as chiseled as the nearby bronze statute of a leaping male dancer.

"Forgive me for being so forward," he said breathlessly, "but I must take the chance."

He took her hands in his, smiling down at her.

Heart pounding, she considered withdrawing her hands. What was he doing, where was this going? And why hadn't she withdrawn her hands yet?

"Will you join me for dinner tonight?" he asked.

"Oh—" She let go then, exhaling. No, dinner was going too far. A duet, a walk; all in good fun. But dinner? Too serious, too deliberate.

She grimaced. "I—"

"It's alright," he said, taking the hint. A sheepish smile. "I jumped the gun, I know it. How about drinks then . . . No? Okay, how about this. . . . Ice cream on the harbor. Just two musicians discussing a shared profession, nothing more."

Drew had just walked past a row of parked scooters when the front door of the post office opened across the street and Kylie stepped out.

He turned his face and ducked around the side of a building, relaxing as he glanced back over his shoulder: she hadn't seen him, and it looked like they were heading for the park.

Without time for consideration, he crossed the busy street and followed at a distance, pulse racing. Maybe a park was the best place to meet up after all, rather than at Edward's house. Though Kylie wasn't the type of person to make a scene, he felt safer in public somehow; doubting she'd be happy to see him. So why not get it over with here? But when to approach? He didn't want to frighten them.

By the looks of things, he assumed Ms. Airoso to be on a mission; walking briskly in her high-heeled sandals, asymmetrical dress swirling about her. The others trailed behind, walking slower. The sight of Mya and Keira made his heart contract—how he longed to sweep them up into his arms this very moment.

Nevertheless, he lingered far behind in the shade of trees, uncertain what to do and feeling like a creeper. He should have just told Kylie his plans to travel here instead of keeping it a secret. This was silly.

The group soon disappeared into the foliage of what he knew to be the koi pond enclosure, and a minute or two passed before Kylie reappeared.

When she did, he took a step backward as though struck.

Some tall, suave-looking man had linked Kylie's arm in his as they strolled away together . . . like a couple.

Avoiding any open spaces where he might be seen, Drew moved through and around groves, trying to keep his wife and the stranger in view without being detected himself. When they stepped off the path near the pergola, he had a direct line of sight but was too far away to hear their voices. His breathing shallowed as the unknown man took both of Kylie's hands in his.

Unable to watch a second longer, Drew turned around and retraced his steps back to the post office with a quick stride, keeping well out of sight. He then began the trek back to his hotel, staring at the sidewalk only while trying to avoid colliding with anyone heading the opposite way. He could hardly breathe.

Who was Kylie with at the park? And had they embraced after he left . . . kissed even? He couldn't bear to watch. He'd travelled all this way only to discover it was actually a romantic getaway for Kylie—with a secret boyfriend. Oh what a fool he'd been.

His throat tightened painfully and he walked even faster, thankful for sunglasses to hide his eyes. Despite the humidity he felt chilled all over.

If not for being in public he would have dropped to his knees then and there—and put his face to his hands.

When Ramiro had asked her about ice cream on the harbor, Kylie consented after only a brief hesitation; figuring it was safe enough being a public place, daylight, and no alcohol involved. She told herself it was a chance to get to know him better and see if he might truly be Pearl's cousin after all. It didn't make any sense that a man would pursue another woman so openly in front of his lover; she must be reading too much into the situation.

They set a time and meeting place, and rejoined Pearl and the girls at the koi pond. Pearl seemed miffed when they returned, as though she disapproved of them going off alone together, but she said nothing. Was it jealousy? Something else?

Ramiro said good-bye and walked away. Pearl's demeanour remained stiff and agitated the whole time they were together at the grocery store, looking for supper supplies. They shared very little conversation besides food talk, and spoke mainly with the children. The bus ride home was a silent one.

During dinner, which Kylie had prepared, she asked her father if he would mind spending the evening with his granddaughters while she went out on her own for a much needed break. Pearl gave Kylie a startled glance as he cheerfully agreed, but he didn't seem to notice.

Kylie cringed inwardly, cheeks warming, and avoided further eye contact. She hated to lie but there was no way she could mention Ramiro to her father. It wasn't a secret really, just far too complicated to explain: he thought Pearl was being unfaithful, and Pearl thought Edward didn't know anything.

Later, when it was time to head out, Pearl came down the stairs in her dressing gown and accosted Kylie at the front door.

"Are you meeting with my cousin?" she asked in a hushed, almost hissing tone of voice.

Kylie maintained a neutral expression but there was no sense denying it. "Yes, but only to chat for a little while. It's not every day I have the opportunity to talk with a fellow musician. We're just going to sit at the marina."

Pearl took a step closer. Her hair was neatly combed but she no longer wore makeup; eyes red and puffy as though she'd been crying. "Please do not go," she said, searching Kylie's face. "It is a mistake."

"Why—is he married?" Her whole body prickled as she waited for a response. Though she still doubted he was Pearl's cousin, engaging another woman right in front of someone he was romantically involved with seemed even more doubtful. There must be another explanation. Besides, what did it even matter? They were just friends.

"He is quite unattached, I promise you that," Pearl said flatly. "However *you* are married. Though he will not care."

A beat passed.

"I know you are lonesome," she went on, "and for all I know, soon to be divorced. Yet this is reckless, can't you see? Ramiro, he is a beautiful-looking man, I do not deny that. He has his charms as well—a voice like silk—those bedroom eyes—they could melt any woman." A line formed in her brow. "So I must speak candidly with you this time. You are being seduced."

Heat coursed through Kylie's body and she jerked the door open. "A man expresses interest in me, so it must be seduction?" She stepped out onto the portico. "My mind, my personality, my musical abilities, all mean nothing?"

Pearl followed, stopping in the door frame, looking pained. "Ramiro has high standards and those things most certainly increase his attraction to you exponentially, yes. He would not give you a second glance if not for your intelligence and gift-edness. Yet you must believe me about his intentions. He is my . . . cousin. I know him like I know myself!"

"Is he really your cousin though? Just tell me that he's not, tell me you're in love with him, or whatever it is . . . and I won't go."

Pearl took a step backward, the color draining from her face. "In love with him? No, no, you have it all wrong. I wish I could explain it to you, but I can not. Please, Kylie. Trust me. It's not too late to cancel." Pursing her lips, she pivoted and shut the door behind her without another word.

Kylie frowned, hesitating.

Then she walked down the driveway. It would be embarrassing to go back inside; it would imply too much and she'd have to make up an excuse to her father. Besides, she didn't want Pearl having power over her like that, especially when everything she said about Ramiro was cryptic and confusing. No, she wasn't going to cancel.

When she reached the road, she called a taxi and sat on a boulder in the shade of a purple orchid tree, hands trembling as she clasped them together on her bare knees. Meeting with Ramiro alone tonight did seem reckless, she had to admit. He was a virtual stranger, it was true.

But.

The man was a magnet.

Did it matter though, him being physically attractive? Should she only associate with plain-looking men? Oh but his eyes, they said it all. When she had first met Drew, he looked at her in the same way. Why lie to herself? Pearl was right . . . Ramiro was definitely pursuing her.

And she wanted him to.

The day she discovered Drew watching porn was the day she stopped feeling attractive. Even long before that day really, as she noticed his waning interest; the pulling away. An affair had seemed unlikely though since he was usually home with the kids while she was out, and his brother typically joined him whenever he went golfing with friends: she knew Joel would never be complicit in such a thing. Nevertheless, she sensed something had changed between them, an invisible barrier set in place. And then, after learning the truth, she automatically looked back over the past year with new lenses, wondering if every kiss, every embrace, had been a lie.

Which woman, which breasts, which body, which face, was he seeing in his mind each time he held her? And when had he become so bored of her in the first place that he sought the vicarious sex of other women? He was still as handsome to her as the day they met; and when she kissed him, she kissed *him*—no one else.

Why hadn't *she* been enough?

A taxi appeared around the bend slowing to a stop in front of her and she climbed into the back seat. Soon palmettos and allspice trees whipped by as the taxi headed for town; houses looking like cupcakes with their white limestone roofs.

Each time Ramiro Airoso gazed at her, she felt desirable, attractive—alluring. He was looking at *her*. Regardless of whatever his past romantic relationships were, she was the current object of his desire. She had no intention of having an affair with him though—for all she knew, he was a porn user as well—but right now, tonight, in Bermuda, she wanted to feel beautiful again . . . if only for a brief while.

Reckless? Maybe. But to resist a sunbeam

after months of being cold?

She paid the taxi driver and got out on Front Street near an ice cream parlor where she was to meet him at eight o'clock.

Though early, he was already there, reclining at a table inside. He stood as she entered, meeting her eyes with a smile and closing the gap between them. They decided on frozen yogurt and ate it while walking to Barr's Bay Park, a waterfront esplanade that overlooked the marina of the Royal Bermuda Yacht Club.

After discarding their cups, they took a regal, balustrade-lined ramp into the park and followed the path down the center. The beginning sunset was already visible in the western sky, swaths of peach and orange on the dusty blue. Coconut palms backdropped wide expanses of greensward; benches evenly distributed along the cement walkway of the water's edge. They chose a bench and sat down.

Conversation so far had been casual, trivial, with an emphasis on music, much like their chat on the railroad trail had been. And as usual, he was laidback and confident; a smooth talker. It put her at ease to not have to grapple for topics. He told her amusing stories and she in turn shared a few of her own.

The frozen yogurts had kept their hands

occupied for much of the walk; a relief for Kylie who didn't want to be seen or recognized by anyone in town who might know her. But now that they sat side by side, he draped his arm over the back of the bench in a classic movie theatre stance. If he had been Drew, leaning into the crook of his shoulder would have been the most natural thing for her to do. Instead she sat with a stiff back, trying to hide her self-consciousness.

Reggae music danced on the breeze from one of the many moored yachts. Water lapped against the docks; gulls alighting on the water here and there.

"Pearl once told me how much she would adore getting married on a boat," he said, staring out at the horizon thoughtfully. "Not a cruise ship, but a big yacht with only her closest friends present. She envisioned them anchoring their boats all around and leaving after the ceremony so that her and Mr. Patterson could enjoy the remainder of the night alone together. It's a rather charming idea, I must confess." A whimsical smile and a sidelong glance. "She said to me, 'I want stars above me and the water surrounding—I want to feel like the only two people in the universe.' " He chuckled. "So then, do you think your father will in fact ever marry her?"

Kylie met his eyes. They were soft and warm, gazing down at her.

It was difficult to picture her father taking such a romantic disposition with a woman—he found outward displays of sentimentality embarrassing—but she hoped him capable. However his comments lately suggested he and Pearl were falling out of love. She wasn't about to tell Ramiro that though. "I don't know his plans," she said instead. "Has Pearl ever been married?" Her father hadn't mentioned his girlfriend's past before and she'd never asked.

"Why yes, twice in fact. The first one was an old highschool friend of mine. He owned a fitness club here on the rock—she had a membership there. But he eventually left her for one of his trainers, the schmuck. A couple years later she married some hairstylist she met through the salon."

"The one she worked at?"

A nod. "He did a lot of international travel though, competing and promoting his work. She felt abandoned, I suppose. Now, as far as I know she ended that one herself."

They stared straight ahead at the view, the mood feeling momentarily solemn.

"He is not at all her type, your father," Ramiro went on, "though as you know, I've never met him in person. I have seen pictures—the notable age difference and . . . level of fitness, if I'm blunt." He shrugged. "But to each their own, as the saying goes."

Should she defend her father? Nah. Truth was, she'd had the same thought herself, many times. They did seem an unlikely pair.

"Can I ask," she said, "and I hope this doesn't seem rude, but why hasn't Pearl ever introduced you to him?"

"Oh, likely incidental." A half smile. "I have only been around for a few months, you see, and before that we went several years unable to see one another. I'm usually only able to visit her during the daytime as well, given my schedule, and that is typically when your father is at work." He looked away, fixing his gaze on a sailboat gliding by.

She assumed he was lying, at least in part, based on her previous conversations with Pearl. This avoidance of Edward was deliberate, not incidental. So why continue to sit here with him without knowing what was being covered up? She knew he wanted to a make a move on her; there was no use pretending about that. Yet despite the unanswered questions, she didn't want to leave the esplanade, let alone the bench. His attention was flattering, intoxicating; though all she had in mind was a bit of magic, nothing more. A taste of romance after months of deprivation. The warmth and sizzle of harmless flirting. They were in a public place after all; it was safe.

The scent of his cologne surrounded her on the breeze, along with the fragrance of nearby flowers. He shifted his position as if trying to get more comfortable and the space between them decreased even more. Goosebumps rose on her skin. Though a balmy night, the temperature had cooled a little with the fading sun. She told herself it was only that. The sky and waters were greycast now, though a few wisps of peach remained. It would soon be dark, save for the many lights of the boats and the lampposts throughout the park.

He made a humorous observation about a seagull perched on a yacht and they laughed and shared a glance. Reggae music continued to play. His gaze lingered after that, eyes beginning to smolder. She looked away, heart racing, breathing shallow.

Without warning his fingertips touched her chin, gently turning her face back toward him.

She breathed in his cologne again; felt heady.

He leaned in, nudging her chin closer, and his lips met hers.

CHAPTER 15

Ramiro pulled her into his arms.

She couldn't stop, couldn't pull away, heart hammering in her chest as they kissed. One taste wasn't enough—she needed more, so much more. How long since she'd been passionately embraced by a man, by Drew?

Drew.

She put her hands on Ramiro's chest, pushing him away as they continued to kiss, until their lips finally broke apart. Her whole body trembled but she managed to stand up without losing her balance.

"I'm sorry," she stammered. "I shouldn't have."

He stood and put his hands in his pockets, completely at ease. "No apology necessary, my dear. It is getting late after all. Why don't we head to the road and I'll hail you a cab, yes?"

It took all her strength to act casual, feeling weak and shaky as they walked side by side, her face flushed.

She was glad for dusk, for the shadows to hide her face. He didn't seem angry though, only disappointed perhaps. It would have been unbearable otherwise. They spoke very little as they waited at the road, and parted amiably enough.

She was soon alone in the backseat of a taxi, staring out the window, cheeks awash with tears.

After arriving home, she opened the gate and walked up the driveway as if in a trance, the moon adding a silver tinge to the tree leaves; flower petals black where they strewed the ground. The window above the front entrance was lit, a chandelier glinting beyond, and the rest of the house dark. She reached the portico and sat down on the steps, leaning against one of the smooth cold columns, a chorus of chirping frogs rising from the woodland.

She breathed in and out slowly, focusing on the scent of cedar in the air and trying to calm down. Never had she felt such a nauseating combination of longing and repulsion.

Ramiro was a stranger. A handsome stranger. She knew nothing of his past, his values, his heart. And what did he know of hers? She looked down at her bare ring finger. He didn't even know she was married. Or did he? The day they met he mentioned the 'pictures on the mantel' . . . one was a wedding portrait. Pearl's words rang through her mind: *He will not care.*

She had kissed a complete stranger . . . walked right into it too—deliberately. Just for a taste, for a thrill; to feel alive again. But instead of it being a balm to her aching heart, she felt raw, feverish even.

She sat on the step for what seemed an hour, staring into the darkness and listening to the night peepers—then got up and went indoors, hoping no trace of tears remained should her father happen to make an appearance and ask about her time.

The hallway was dim beyond the entrance, and the library dark when she peeked in. It seemed that everyone had already retired. She went upstairs and noticing a light under her father's bedroom door, gave it a rap. He poked his head out, wearing a housecoat; a flat screen TV glowing on the far wall of the room. They exchanged a few words and she found herself lying a second time, claiming she'd had a nice evening and making no mention of Ramiro. Edward showed no signs of suspicion. They said good-night and he shut the door. She then took soft steps into the girls' room and found them both asleep; their figures contoured by moonlight. Standing at the bedside of each in turn, she fixed tangled blankets, adjusted stuffies, and smoothed away hair from their foreheads; her heart in her throat as she looked down at them tenderly.

Minutes later she was climbing in under her own bedsheets, face freshly washed and night clothes on. She lay on the left side of the bed staring at the pillow next to her; crisp and smooth, untouched. If Drew were there, already asleep, she might have snuggled up against him, breathing in his scent and holding him close.

She shut her eyes and Ramiro was kissing her again on the park bench at dusk.

The next morning, having spent a long night mulling over what he'd seen, processing, Drew decided to carry through with his original plan to present himself at his father-in-law's house, rather than just immediately returning to Ontario. He would request shared time with his daughters and nothing more.

His tenuous hope of reconciling with Kylie snapped like a dry twig when he saw her with another man in the park.

What's more, if she'd journeyed here to vacation with a new boyfriend, the sudden appearance of her estranged husband was sure to cause dismay—hostility even. If he'd only known. Was this why she often went out in the evenings when he spent time with Mya and Keira? He thought it was simply to avoid him; now he wondered if the affair had been going on all along. He'd waited week after week, giving her all the space she needed, hoping she still loved him enough to eventually reconcile—but divorce seemed inevitable if she was already involved with someone else.

Having dressed in a T-shirt and shorts, Drew finished breakfast, left the hotel, and went out onto the street to await the next pink transit bus.

The sky was overcast, palm leaves droopy in the muggy air. He tugged down his baseball cap and paced a little, heartbeat picking up a notch whenever he thought of what the next hour might bring. A couple of scooters whizzed by. He stared across the street at the harbor, then at the hazy horizon. A day ago, his only fear had been how angry Kylie might be with him for showing up without advanced notice. How naïve. Now he feared the unknown reality he'd stumbled upon, which would soon become more dreadfully clear. Was this how Kylie felt when she first discovered his secret porn usage? Shocked . . . gutted?

The bus arrived and he filed in behind several other people and sat in an aisle seat, feeling cramped and losing his balance every few minutes on the winding roads. He was queasy by the time the gates of Edward's estate appeared around a bend; though from the turbulent drive or his nerves, he couldn't be sure. After exiting the bus, he went to the driveway and stood at the gates for a while next to the purple orchid tree; drawing in deep breaths and willing himself to calm. At length, he pressed the intercom button on the passcode pad.

The housekeeper answered—audibly startled when he introduced himself.

"Shall I let Kylie know that you're here before you reach the door?" she asked in a near whisper. "She's on the terrace with the children."

"No, it's okay. And if it's all the same, Connie, why don't I just walk around the back?"

"Alright then," she said, sounding uncertain. "Best of luck to you."

He grimaced but said nothing. The gates opened and he made his way up the driveway, taking his time. It seemed a lifetime ago since he was last here, though everything looked much the same. When he reached the palmetto amongst a row of cedar trees at the side of the Georgian home, he stood staring at it, remembering. It was just tall enough to stand beneath and had fan-shaped fronds, the trunk covered in the cross-hatched petiole bases of former leaves. He continued walking. The ocean was in sight now: slate beneath a cloudy sky. He went down the slope and the terrace came into view as he rounded the side. Kylie was sitting bent over the table under the parasol with what looked like a Sudoku puzzle; her back to him. She hadn't heard his footfall on the grass. The girls were on the lawn halfway between the house and the beach, blowing bubbles toward the sea. They didn't see him either.

He stood still and watched, saying a prayer inwardly for strength and guidance; then said her name softly.

Kylie turned in her seat and jumped up so fast the chair fell backwards, clattering on the flagstone. Mya and Keira looked over at the sound and squealed with joy, setting down their bubble dispensers and racing toward Drew. Within seconds they had him tackled, his baseball hat falling to the grass. He gave them his full attention until they settled down—and they returned to their bubbles when he told them he needed to talk to their mother for a moment. He retrieved his hat and looked back toward Kylie, holding it in his hands.

She had righted the chair and stood staring,

as though frozen. He approached, stopping on the flagstone next to a flower urn; leaving a meter of space between them. She wore white shorts and a teal tank top, her curls extra flouncy in the humid air. A pink flush mantled her cheeks, her eyes slightly narrowed. His throat tightened as he thought of the mysterious man he'd seen her with —the man who looked like he'd just stepped out of a Calvin Kline ad—how he'd taken Kylie's hands in his and gazed down into her husky blue eyes . . . and how she hadn't resisted.

"How long have you been here?" she asked, voice sounding choked.

"Since Sunday."

Something sparked in her eyes. Anger? No. Fear?

"I'm sorry." He frowned, gripping the hat tighter. "I'd just like to spend time with the girls . . . didn't wanna lose half the summer, I miss them too much. . . . " He cleared his throat. "I'll stay out of your way, I promise." She remained deadpan. "And I uh, thought maybe we could take turns with them," he went on, nodding toward the girls.

He told her what hotel he was staying at, and fell silent.

Kylie hesitated, unsure what to say next. She felt completely stunned by his presence: one moment he was in Ontario, the next, here. It was as if he'd teleported.

And he was as tall and handsome as ever too, his shoulders strong and broad, black hair trimmed short around the sides and longer on top. But there was a look of reservation in his green eyes —a reserve that even during their separation hadn't been there. They weren't cold or hard, just cloaked. He was holding back as one might do with an acquaintance. Being polite yet giving no evidence of wanting to take things further. If not for this remarkable change in his eyes, she might have assumed he was there to ask for her forgiveness again.

Instead he looked . . . done.

Impassive.

Yet only a few days had gone by since he asked over the phone if she still loved him. Did she completely misinterpret that conversation? Had he been seeking closure rather than hope?

A second blush prickled her cheeks, pulse quickening. His hotel wasn't in view of Barr's Bay Park, but he was already on the Island when Ramiro kissed her . . .

"How long will you be staying?" She kept her voice measured, even.

"Two weeks."

She struggled to keep her expression neutral, swallowing.

"If you want, I can return to the hotel and come back later."

She put her hand on the back of the cedar chair, lifting her chin a little. "No, if you'll stay outside with the girls right now and give me a few minutes to think things through . . . we'll set up some kind of a schedule."

Without another glance, she went into the house through the library and into the hallway, nearly colliding with Pearl, who was leaving the kitchen with a bottle of water. Wearing workout clothes, her hair was damp; a sheen of sweat on her brow. Her face was pale and she looked ready to collapse.

"Pearl, something has happened," Kylie explained. "Andrew is here—in the backyard. He flew in on Sunday, didn't tell me his plans and . . . well now he's here." She hitched her thumb over her shoulder. "Out there with the kids. Surprise!" A half-hearted laugh.

Pearl's eyes widened and she seemed almost frightened. She put a hand on the door frame as though to steady herself. "Is he going to be staying here?"

"Oh no, no, he's got a hotel room. But he's going to be coming around to spend time with Mya and Keira."

"During the day, here?"

Kylie narrowed her eyes a little. "Yes, but you won't need to entertain, don't worry. We are . . . going to be staying out of each other's way. He will likely take them on outings around the island." It was all she could do to keep emotion from cracking up her voice. Her eyes stung.

Pearl unscrewed the lid of her water bottle, taking a delicate sip, returning the lid. "This is going to be difficult," she said frankly, making eye contact.

Why? Was she afraid that having another witness to Ramiro's visits might increase Edward's chance of finding out? Kylie held back a grimace at the thought. Her father already knew.

"I never dreamed he'd come here, Pearl, but he does have a right to be with his daughters—I've been hoarding them and it's not fair. I'm so sorry though, I feel like I'm imposing all over again."

Pearl massaged her left temple as though long-suffering. "I am sure Edward will not mind it —you are his daughter after all." She headed for the staircase then, ascending.

Kylie followed her upstairs and went to her own room, going straight for the window that faced the beach. She didn't want to be caught spying but hoped for a quick glance at her husband. The children were still on the grass, blowing bubbles—Keira running around trying to pop them before they floated away. Drew didn't look up at the house, so Kylie remained next to the drape and watched him freely. She supposed he'd left his hat on the table, and was glad of it: she wanted to see his face again, the curve of his lips when he smiled adoringly at the children. How long had it been since that smile was for her? Since they'd shared a smile . . . It seemed ages. And those green eyes, how she missed them.

Suppressed tears began to well. Finally surrendering, she left the window and collapsed on the bed to weep. Then, when she could weep no more, she went to the ensuite to wash her face, apply fresh makeup, and hide all signs of crying before heading back outside.

They saw her coming and turned around in anticipation but Drew's eyes remained guarded, his expression courteous with nothing showing beneath. Even still she might have attempted an embrace, but her arms felt stiff at her sides—from the memory of kissing another man just the night before.

She stopped a few feet away from him and stood in place, struggling to hold eye contact for more than a couple seconds at a time. In a voice much colder than intended, she robotically discussed a schedule with him covering the next two weeks. He then hugged his daughters good-bye and gave her a formal nod, taking his leave with the plan of returning in the morning to pick up the children.

He retrieved his baseball cap from the table as he passed by it and she bit her lower lip—holding back from calling out to him, from begging him to stay. With a final wave to the children, he disappeared around the side of the house. She shivered, chilled despite the humidity. But rather than a feeling of sunshine going behind clouds, she'd glimpsed her lost heart and watched him walk away with it.

At dinnertime, Kylie informed her father of Drew's presence on the Island. He seemed pleased to hear it, despite her lack of enthusiasm. Pearl said very little, likely due to her vested interests, and kept her focus on slicing her unadorned food into tiny bites. She was either ruminating, or pretending to, while listening to every word spoken. Kylie hardly ate at all.

Halfway through dinner, Trey arrived home, joining them in the dining room when he realized supper had been served. With Kylie and Pearl saying so little, however, Edward seemed anxious to make conversation with someone, any-one, and was soon imposing himself on Trey, who bristled under the fixed attention. As entertaining as their father could be, he didn't like gloomy silences, of which Trey seemed to excel, so he com-pensated by nit-picking. He wanted to know where the boy had been all day . . . what he'd been up to all week for that matter . . . how his job-hunting was going . . . and "Dammit, why so cagey all the time? Have you even handed out resumes—is there even a resume in existence *to* be handed out?" Mya and Keira were all ears at this point, eyes wide. They understood by the increasing stridency of Grandpa's tone that Trey was in the hotseat.

Trey tossed his fork on the tabletop with a clatter and dropped out of his seat, cussing under his breath as he left the room.

Edward glared after him red-faced, shoul-ders back and buttons looking close to popping. He said nothing but cleared his throat and leaned for-ward to concentrate on eating; likely trying to com-pose himself. He took a second helping and when he'd finally finished every morsel, even wiping away the remnants of gravy on his plate with the last piece of dinner roll, he suddenly turned to the children with a jolly smile and silly story.

Only then could Kylie begin to relax.

Her experience of Edward would never be quite the same as Trey's, but she didn't doubt that if she'd stayed in Bermuda as a teen, she too would have felt the pressure to be productive, to make something great of herself, to please her father—one of the most ambitious men she'd ever known. She did feel it from afar at times though, when he urged her not to settle in her job as a music teacher but to keep working toward an orchestra. Or when he heaped on the praise for her musical talent but always with a nip at the end: the reminder to keep bettering herself. It often left her with a lingering feeling of insecurity, of not being quite enough as she was. More than once she'd wondered if he would be as warm and affectionate with her if she didn't have any particular talent to interest him with, or if she'd lived with him during her teen years. She could only imagine what that pressure had been like, and still was, for Trey; since he hid all of his aspirations from his father. Did he receive any affection at all?

Maybe Trey simply preferred to be seen as a freeloader rather than have all the fun vampired out of his cooking. No doubt as soon as his father thought he might have a talent for such things, there'd be the pressure to impress and ever improve. Still, why not at least get a day job to lessen the negative attention from his father? Though maybe even with a job, Edward might persist in pushing Trey toward college or university; each stepping stone he took requiring advancement to the next.

Later that night, while Kylie was getting Mya and Keira in their pajamas, she noticed her brother leaving his bedroom, head tucked down and a duffel bag over his shoulder.

He didn't look her way and she wondered where he was going—wishing she was closer to him, that she knew him better. But they simply lived too far apart for that to be possible. Then again, living in the same house didn't guarantee closeness either. The three of them—Trey, Edward and Pearl—all seemed to be living separate lives.

After spending time reading to the girls and saying their bedtime prayers, Kylie went downstairs and found her father alone in the library watching TV. She joined him and tried to immerse herself in the program, some made-for-tv thriller, but failed. He didn't seem interested in talking though, so she scrolled her phone instead, chatting with a few friends back home but feeling increasingly bored. Eventually Edward hefted himself out of his seat and went for a refill of his scotch, collecting his cigar box as well. She accepted a glass of red wine from him and watched as he set his drink on a coaster and prepared the cigar, cutting and lighting the tip before sinking back down into the wingback chair.

During the next commercial break, he turned toward her, leaning on the arm of the chair and looking thoughtful. "Andrew is welcome to stay here, by the way," he said. "He doesn't need to stay in a hotel."

"Dad, we're not together."

"I know, I know." He waved his cigar. "But should you decide to give it another go . . . " A pointed look.

She sighed. If only it were that easy.

"Well, what's stopping you then?"

"Everything? Besides, he says he's just here to share time with the girls, doesn't want to lose 'half the summer' with them. His words. He made no indication that his visit has anything to do with me in the slightest. He also seemed completely closed off when he talked to me. I mean—more than ever before. I think something has changed."

The commercial break ended and Edward turned his attention back to the show without responding.

She spent the next ten minutes brooding, nursing her wine, and loathing the feeling of embarrassment and anxiety that came along with opening up to someone only to be ignored or invalidated.

"Maybe it's just that the ball's in your court, sweetheart," he said suddenly as the next commercial break began. He twisted to face her. "Maybe he's waiting for an indication from *you*."

Her throat tightened and she looked away.

But I've kissed another man.

How could she ever confess that to Drew? *Honey, I messed around with some guy last night . . . want to get back together?*

She tossed back the last burgundy sip.

Her father, who'd been watching her with a look of scrutiny, offered a refill, and she accepted.

"You know," he said after, sitting back down and retrieving his cigar from the ashtray next to him, "Pearl has gone out tonight. . . . She's not asleep, as you may have assumed." He rubbed his trimmed goatee slowly. "Do you know if she ever meets with . . . that man . . . elsewhere, and not just at the house? I'm not here during the day so I can only guess at how she spends her time."

Kylie hesitated, unsure how to respond, heartbeat picking up a notch. "I need to tell you, Dad, she does insist that Ra—this man—really is her cousin. I think I might have been mistaken in doubting that—and I'm worried I gave you the wrong impression!" She swallowed. "But to answer your question, there was the once when they played a game of tennis together, going somewhere afterwards, and another time when he picked her up at the house to 'run errands' of some sort." Heat climbed her face. "And just yesterday he met up with us briefly at Queen Elizabeth's park in the afternoon, but all she did was give him a book. . . . Then we left."

"A book? What book?"

"I'm not sure, some paperback. I didn't see the title."

"Interesting." He took a pull on his cigar. "Because the past few months she's been attending a book club at a friend's house, weekly. I never asked for details, though I do remember being surprised by it. She isn't much of a reader, you see." A smoky exhale. "I figured it was a pretext for a bunch of women to get together and gab while feeling intellectual. Heh. But I suppose the whole thing must have been a ruse—of course he isn't her cousin.

"See this is what happens when you're complacent like me," he said, tapping his cigar at her. "Everything goes to crap. I didn't learn anything from your mother and I'm afraid Pearl has all the same complaints that she did. You can't teach an old dog new tricks and all that drivel. I don't know what Pearl ever saw in me anyway, it's quite baffling. No, I'm serious. When we first met, I felt ridiculous flirting with such a beautiful woman, totally bonkers, but she encouraged it, so I kept going. And then when she returned my affections —Blimey! Seemed too good to be true, I admit. So, I figured hey let's ride this wave as long as it lasts— that was my attitude. Still is, really. Take it or leave it, this is who I am." He turned back to the TV without waiting for Kylie to respond, adjusting his shoulders and getting comfortable again.

She held back a biting remark, sipping her drink hotly and glaring at the fireplace instead.

How could her father be aware that his girlfriend of five years was so unhappy, but not bother to make any changes for her? Didn't he care that he might lose her, just as he had lost Kylie's mother? Or maybe he did care but felt change was too hard. That seemed more likely, especially with his comment about riding the wave. Even though nothing could impede the man from excelling in his business endeavors, he did have a tendency to quail when confronted with his relational shortcomings.

Drew hadn't been complacent or neglectful like her father though.

At least, not at first.

But because she struggled with expressing strong feelings, she felt embarrassed when he tried to get her talking about her depression—and because she was depressed, his attentiveness therefore became increasingly annoying. She wanted to either get out of the house to escape her gloomy thoughts or be left alone to play the violin; not dredge everything up.

He eventually stopped trying, and little by little, withdrew.

In the beginning it was a relief though, like the lifting of a burden: they could be friends again without her feeling exposed, just as she was with her girlfriends and mother. In time, however, his waning affections began to feel more like abandonment. She realized she did crave a deeper emotional connection with him. But by then it seemed too late: she didn't know how to reverse the situation. How could she initiate the very thing she found so difficult to reciprocate? And why couldn't Drew have lost himself in something benign, like golf, as she always did with the violin? All through their separation she'd been thinking if only he had been more patient and waited a little longer—until she was feeling like herself again—the whole porn thing might have been avoided. Now it seemed maybe not. Even without porn their relationship probably would have continued to erode . . . albeit at a slower pace.

And maybe turning to her violin wasn't as benign as she thought.

Why had she assumed that the lack of emotional intimacy between her and Drew would reverse itself naturally once her depression ceased? The intimacy had never quite been there to begin with. She saw that now. Those first few years of marriage when babysitters weren't needed, when the high of the honeymoon phase still ran strong, she enjoyed spending time with him; her favorite companion. They had such fun together and affection was easy. She wasn't particularly depressed in those days either, so her cheerfulness and passion likely created the illusion that she was much more open with him than she really was. Though she hadn't acknowledged it to herself then, she sensed he needed more communion of the heart than she'd been willing to give. He always fulfilled her need for affection, but after years of her avoiding being open-hearted with him in return—his need—he must have felt increasingly rejected. She didn't feel the already present lack—a lack he did feel—until he pulled away.

Kylie glanced over at her father.

The light flickered on his face as he stared at the TV, puffing on his cigar, entranced by the show. He must care about Pearl, probably loved her too, just as Kylie had genuinely loved Drew. But he was coping the same way he always had: by ignoring his problems, seeking distraction, and leaving Pearl to her own devices. Kylie had to admit she'd done the same thing with Drew—though with her violin more than anything else.

And with Edward now having admitted to taking his common-law wife for granted, the whole picture of Drew was changing in Kylie's mind—like shuffling a deck of cards and looking at a fresh hand. Things appeared differently than they had a day before.

For the past four months she believed her husband had lost all interest in her physically; that lust had propelled him to covet other women. Now that seemed overly simplistic. Drew had been lonely, so lonely. And the natural yearning for passion, for the delight of romance and eros, had led him to an intoxicating decoy.

She thought of Ramiro, remembered how her stomach fluttered whenever he looked at her with unveiled attraction, her skin tingling whenever he touched her arm. And Monday night, the sun dipping under the horizon, reggae music, his spicy cologne and kindled eyes; the electric charge when his lips pressed against hers. . . . But though she responded physically in the moment, it wasn't

Ramiro she wanted. Not really. His eyes, his mouth. Not hers. He neither had the face of her love, nor the hands. Even the musk was all wrong. It was Drew she still yearned for, only Drew.

Her hands were cold and clammy in her lap, wine glass long empty on the end table next to her.

Having zero interest in the show Edward was watching, Kylie said good-night to her father, who murmured a response without looking; and she left the room, heading for the kitchen to wash her glass.

The kitchen was dark aside from dim lighting over the cooking range, but it was enough to see the sink, so she didn't turn on any other lights. She set the glass in the drying rack just as a key could be heard turning the bolt in the front entrance door.

Kylie moved into the shadows near the opening to the hallway, and waited.

It was Pearl.

She watched as the woman went to the closet and put her purse away, retrieving two items from it before heading up the staircase.

In her hands was a box of Band-Aids and an old paperback.

CHAPTER 16

Wednesday and Thursday crawled by.

Drew took the kids both days and Kylie found his demeanour overly formal. He had little to say to her, besides comparing itineraries, and didn't attempt any small talk. Though she searched his face and body language for any sign of connection, any hint of affection, she found none. He was completely walled up. It was hard to believe that this man, still her husband—who she at one time could sidle up to, embrace, kiss, take the hand of—was like a stranger now, unapproachable physically.

He wasn't hers anymore.

Ramiro made no appearances at all, a relief to Kylie, who resorted to passing the hours in the music room, playing the violin until her fingers ached—though it did nothing to soothe her frayed nerves. If anything, it seemed to exacerbate them now. Pearl continued to spend a good two hours a day in the exercize room, followed by several more in her bedroom, skipping tea time and retiring early after supper. In the evenings a sullen Edward watched TV in the library and Kylie sat with him; scrolling her phone, reading random books from the shelves, and drumming her fingers.

Thursday afternoon she spent teatime alone in the shade of the garden, staring toward the turquoise sea, absently watching as distant boats floated by. Presently, the laughter of children sounded from the front of the house, rousing her, and she figured it must be Drew returning with Mya and Keira.

She set down her China cup with a clink, half full of tepid tea, and walked around the side of the house to greet them. The trio emerged from under the canopy of the last two trees as she rounded the corner. Drew walked casually behind the girls, looking dapper; sunglasses obscuring his face, though he wore no hat this time.

He stopped a few feet away from Kylie and gave what seemed a polite smile, not removing the shades. They began to talk about how his time with the children had been that afternoon; his voice sounding guarded. In an undertone, she thought back over all the weeks prior when he'd tried unsuccessfully to have a heart to heart with her about the separation. When the barrier between them—the porn—had seemed insurmountable to her. Yes, he went to counselling and claimed he was staying accountable through software, among other things. She believed that. And he was genuinely sorry too: she didn't doubt that either. So why hadn't it been enough? What more could he have done to make amends? She was beginning to think that what she wanted from Drew was the one thing she could never have, that no one could have.

Security of the future.

She wanted the assurance that he would never backslide, never regress. And maybe that's why up until now she hadn't fully forgiven him; hating the thought of being duped again some day.

Drew said good-bye to the children then, giving them hugs and kisses, and then turned to give Kylie a nod and wave before strolling off. She followed the girls up the steps to the portico and stood watching, her hand on a pillar, until he got all the way to the bottom of the canopied driveway and was gone from sight.

Then she felt deflated.

Gutted.

Longed to run all the way down the drive-way until she caught up with him—and then?

Perhaps only because he still seemed in love with her the past few months, so contrite, she hadn't felt an urgency to make a decision. But now that he was acting closed and aloof, fear swelled in her heart, throat feeling dry. What if she'd waited too long and he no longer wanted to try again?

That evening Pearl left the house after supper and Kylie wondered if the reason she hadn't seen Ramiro was because Pearl was going to him now, to keep him away from the house. Or perhaps he didn't want to see Kylie anymore after being turned down; though he hadn't shown any outward offense at the time. Either way, she was glad for his absence, dreading a situation in which he might show up at the house at the same time as Drew.

After a fitful, prayer-filled night with little sleep, she awoke early the next morning to the muted sounds of Edward and Pearl quarreling in their bedroom, though she couldn't make out the words. At breakfast time Edward announced that he wouldn't be home that evening but planned to meet up with his buddy Lightbourne at the golf course for dinner and drinks. Whether this was pre-planned or a result of his argument with Pearl, she could only guess.

Trey arrived unexpectedly in the early afternoon, on his own, with a duffel bag full of laundry.

"Dad won't be home till late tonight," Kylie told him as they passed each other in the hallway. "Any chance you might like to stay and cook supper for us?" She raised an eyebrow, smiled.

He paused, looked thoughtful. Ran a hand through his tumbling curls. "Hey you know, might as well, sis. Here all afternoon anyway." He pointed toward the nearby laundry room; shrugged. "Plus Cassidy's got classes tonight." He gazed at her shyly then. "Thank you."

"For what?"

"For asking. It means a lot."

She pushed his shoulder.

They spent the rest of the afternoon together and once again, he let his nieces help with the dinner prep. Kylie couldn't remember a time when he'd ever been so talkative with her before. He was beginning to open up; and she hoped, beginning to trust her.

"You know what I like about you?" he said at one point, joining her in the dining room while she was setting the table. His curls hung down over one eye. "I'm not getting the same vibe from you that I get from dad."

"Vibe?"

"Yeah, that feeling that he wants to like

me . . . but not until I've first done this or accomplished that. But you . . . you're like Cassidy that way. I feel alright as is."

She didn't know what to say, was too choked up with emotion, so she hugged him instead. He gave her an awkward pat on the back in return and she laughed.

After first learning from Cassidy that her brother used porn, it was tempting to write him off as a lost cause, a typical male. All that anger and disgust she felt—the disappointment, the cynicism —though she realized her reaction was more of a projection than anything else. It was Drew she was upset with, not Trey. But now here was a young man who was so much more than his vice. He had a tender heart, a heart he kept hidden behind a sullen shield, like his eyes behind curls. If she hadn't accidentally found him cooking in the middle of the night, would she ever have had the chance to get to know him? They'd exchanged nothing but small talk over the past decade. She figured it was the distance between them—the literal distance. But he took great pains to hide himself from Edward as well. On the few occasions when Kylie had witnessed him loosening up with their father, Edward had seemed oblivious to it. Would he ever see this side of his son, or would the two of them forever continue to mirror one another's critical expectations?

With supper ready and set out on hot plates, Mya went upstairs to retrieve Pearl, who'd spent the entire day in her bedroom, and they returned to the dining room together a couple of minutes later. Pearl was wearing slippers and her plum pajamas, her face strikingly pale in contrast. Bruising under her eyes suggested she'd just woken up and hadn't had time to apply any coverup. And though her hair was combed, there was a haggard look about her, hands tremulous as she sipped at a glass of water.

Trey seemed to notice it too, glancing at her obliquely from time to time, but neither he nor Kylie attempted to engage her in any conversation. Her body language made it clear that she was only there to eat, though she barely ate at all: slicing her food into tiny pieces, moving them around, and chewing as though in a trance. She might as well have been eating alone for she paid no attention to anyone, not even the giggling, garrulous children.

Drew left the restaurant he'd dined in, and stepped outside onto the sidewalk, blinking as his eyes adjusted to the brightness.

He waited a moment for a lull in traffic and jogged across the street, slowing his pace when he reached the other side, heading toward Queen Elizabeth Park behind the post office. He still hadn't gotten used to having supper alone, even after four months of doing so. A trio of young women near his solitary table had cast him many subtle glances, or what they thought were subtle, and he noticed. The sweeping away of lashes whenever he looked up, the little smiles and knowing looks they gave one another. He was used to this; knew he was attractive. But the thought of being fully single again some day nauseated him. He would give anything to have his wife back—to have Kylie back—the love of his life.

He went through the open iron gates of the park and wandered to the place where he had witnessed Kylie with the unknown stranger.

The evening sun spread long shadows across the walkway and he sat down on a bench, staring ahead at the sculpture of a leaping dancer. A blossoming tree the color of vermilion blazed beyond it in the distance. He looked to the left of the statue, settling his gaze on the area of grass between the bush and the lamppost—and the couple came into view again like an apparition. Kylie looking up at the guy with that half-shy expression she used to give Drew when they were dating. Did they embrace after he left? His stomach contracted.

Whoever the man was, he was stupidly handsome; if he'd been sitting in the same restaurant that night too, the trio of women wouldn't have given Drew a second glance.

Yes, stupidly handsome. And all the shock of seeing such a specimen with his wife: the instant insecurity, the shattering of confidence. The jealousy. The anguish. His heart twisting and churning in pain and loss. Was this how Kylie felt when she discovered he'd been watching porn? All those stupidly beautiful women, as they must have seemed to her, as they'd once seemed to him. Until they didn't anymore, until they all ran together like a blur, not a hint of individuality. Two-dimensional. The only woman he'd ever revered, had ever loved, was Kylie. Her unique mind, her spirit, matchless in all the world. And her body, once so precious to him—all the sacred intimacy of sharing something with her, and she with him, that no one else was privy to—he'd traded in, tossed in, for an endless stream of generic bodies.

Drew gripped his hands together between his knees, shoulders slumping. Yes, he'd been obsessed with it for a time, jittery, anxious, high. Intoxicated during, hungover after. Like being under a spell—a curse. And no satiation or afterglow to speak of, just wretched guilt, regret, nausea. Fear. A drowning sensation. And whenever he and Kylie made love . . . it was like a traffic jam in his brain, image after image vying for his attention. He couldn't see her, his eyes were blinded. She'd been blotted out for a year. There, but invisible.

He ran both hands through his hair, damp from the heat, and leaned back in the bench. After a few months of abstinence and counselling, of prayer and getting right with God, all that the torrent of imagery, of novelty, was slowing down . . . fading . . . dissipating. His mind, calming. Unlike before when the diet was steady, he now exercized control over the memories, starving them, ignoring them; his eyesight gradually being restored. Though he couldn't delete what he'd seen, he could keep Kylie in his central focus. The lust that for a time had grown so monstrous, had returned to a normal libido. His self-control was back, and subsequently, his inner peace.

But his heart was broken.

Saturday morning Edward announced at breakfast that he wanted to take everyone to Horseshoe Bay Beach for a picnic lunch, Pearl included. It was a sunny day and Kylie's turn with the kids, so she readily agreed, figuring it was better to go on an outing than to mope around the house.

They arrived late morning and set up seaside with towels, umbrella, beach-bum chairs, and a cooler with drinks and food. Edward and the kids were soon splashing together in the shallows and Pearl asked Kylie if she'd like to take a stroll together with her for a while before sunbathing. They let Edward know their plan and were soon off.

Though Pearl wore light makeup, the foundation was again heavy beneath her eyes, a hint of gray showing through. Like Kylie, she wore a pareo skirt around her bikini, along with a sunhat. Instead of going to the coves, they went to the opposite side of the beach and climbed the pathways leading up to a rock cliff. When they reached a high area with an overarching view of both the beach and the ocean, they took a seat next to each other amongst the rocks and shrubs. The curving beach below was a blushing pink, the water a gradient of emerald and turquoise. Edward and the children were only a couple of inches tall from this vantage point.

"He is a good grandfather, yes?" Pearl gave Kylie a sidelong glance and a half smile; her seating position graceful, almost regal.

"He really is."

"It was indeed his playfulness that first caught my eye about him," Pearl went on. "Everyone else around was stiff and formal while he was at ease. I am certain he is quite capable of charming an entire room. It is his gift." Another half smile. "We met at a barbecue—did you know that? That is how he became my broker, in fact. Now I am going to be frank with you, Kylie. I was not attracted to him at first—physically—yet I felt so happy in his presence I soon developed a fast-growing fondness for him. I looked forward to our meetings more and more each time. Then one day I realized I was in love with him. On that day he instantly became the most attractive man I knew."

She paused a moment. "You are probably wondering why I am telling you these things, as they are indeed personal and I do not usually speak with people so openly." She met Kylie's gaze again, adjusted her sunhat. "It is because I need you to understand my . . . situation."

Kylie nodded, feeling uneasy, heartbeat picking up a notch.

"A few years after your father and I became a couple," she continued, "I began to realize that he did not wish to marry me. I thought to myself that if he will not marry me, he does not truly love me. I am a possession but nothing more. If marriage is too risky of an investment for him, a broker, then there must be something flawed within me. I am sufficient to keep, but not good enough to be his wife." She looked down at her tanned knees, glistening in the sunlight. "You may not know this, but I have twice been married before."

"Dad never mentioned it, no, but Ramiro, he—"

"Ramiro?" Pearl's eyes flashed. "He had no right to tell you." She pursed her lips, exhaled. "I thought it was going to be different with Ed—with your father—because he was not . . . he was not physically fit, as were my ex-husbands. That was the main thing, and I thought it was key. I am ashamed to admit this to you, or to anyone, but I thought that he consequently would be afraid of losing me, and would thus dote on me. I therefore anticipated a life together where I could eat freely as he did and no longer worry about maintaining a perfect weight. Does that make sense to you? I could relax and be laid back just like him. I did not want to become overweight, of course, but I did not want to be like this anymore either." She made a sweeping gesture at her figure.

"I dreamed of only having to exercize for half of an hour a day rather than two hours, and perhaps putting on a few pounds as well without any fear or shame. I wanted a weight that was more manageable. Anything less than—this—was completely out of the question with my ex-husbands. That is why I thought my life was going to be different with Ed, with your father. Instead it ended up being precisely the same."

"All because he never proposed?"

A slight nod. "I think he grew accustomed to me and therefore reduced his efforts to engage—to 'woo,' as they say. He was no longer as warm and welcoming with me as he was at first." She looked pensive. "I began to notice that whenever I was not feeling well—when I was moody or glum—he withdrew from me. He secluded himself. He seemed nervous when I was not happy, and yet the affection and attention always returned when I became cheerful again!"

"I hope you don't mind me asking, but do you also get nervous when he's the moody one?"

"Yes, that I do indeed." A sidelong glance. "I worry that I have maybe done something to upset him, so I look for clues that he still loves me. And what I find is that he praises my looks more than anything else, when he is giving me attention. I do not know if there is anything else about me that he actually likes." She looked away. "My current figure is therefore what I must always preserve, if I wish to be loved. It would seem that no man can love me apart from that."

Edward did have a tendency to do that,

Kylie had to agree; he did put too much emphasis on one obvious asset of a person while seldom mentioning the less superficial ones. Like praising Kylie's musical talent or Drew's golfing skills. Maybe it was a crutch for him, a go-to when he was anxious to express admiration: to praise the most obvious attribute. But did her father really only love Pearl for her figure and nothing more? Surely his heart was much too big for that. No, it seemed much more likely to Kylie that he struggled to express his true feelings to people, hiding behind flattery and charisma instead. Easier to compliment someone in a general way than to be vulnerable with them. Like Kylie, he seemed to be embarrassed by anything sentimental in nature.

"I have a secret, Kylie," Pearl said suddenly, "and I wish with all of my heart that I could share it with Edward."

Kylie's pulse quickened again, hands growing clammy.

"However, there is no one I can talk to about it apart from Ramiro. He is family." Another sidelong glance, this time as if to read Kylie's expression before continuing. "The reason that I admit all of this to you, Kylie, is because I know that you have noticed certain things about me during your visit. You have been speculating about it in your attempt to understand."

The memory of Ramiro's kiss Monday night came flooding in and Kylie blushed, hoping the shade of her sunhat would hide it. Though they sat in a wide open space, she felt claustrophobic and panicky; eager for the conversation to be over.

"For example," Pearl went on, "you know that I have been ill, and you know that I meet with Ramiro only when your father is away from home. These two things are facts but the truth is that I am completely faithful to your father and always have been. Ramiro truly is family. However, just as I can not tell Edward my secret, I can not tell you either." There was that pensive look again. "It is . . . far too complicated." She pivoted on the rock, maintaining her graceful posture but facing Kylie directly now. "There is something that you and I have in common though, and I would like to talk to you about that."

Kylie clasped her hands together to keep from fidgeting, and straightened her back, waiting.

"You and I share the same faith. As your father recently mentioned to you, I have indeed converted to Anglicanism, though I was never a practising Catholic. Connie invited me to her church one weekend and I surprised myself by feeling interested. I agreed to go. Now, you might say that I converted out of desperation—and there is indeed truth in that—but I did feel drawn to Jesus Christ in a way that I never had before. I wanted to begin living my life differently. My hope was to find . . . healing . . . yet I am still suffering. Oh dear, you look alarmed. No, I do not have a terminal illness, I promise you." She hesitated a moment as though choosing her words carefully. "Nevertheless, I do not know how much longer I can endure this . . . this condition." A pained look. "Please Kylie—will you pray for me?"

She nodded, wishing Pearl would share more specific details; she was dying to know what the ailment, the "condition" was. It was understandable though. Whatever the secret was, Kylie most likely wouldn't be able to keep it from her father, and Pearl just couldn't risk that.

But if it wasn't an affair or a terminal illness, what could it possibly be? An eating disorder and exercize addiction seemed too obvious—that is, not at all a secret. Surely Edward was bright enough to have noticed his girlfriend's habits in that regard. No, it had to be something else.

The reappearing box of Band-Aids came to mind.

Pearl continued to talk about Christianity and when Edward and the girls left the water to retrieve their towels, she stood up; as though that was what she'd been waiting for. She signaled an abrupt close to their conversation by heading for the pathway that lead down the cliff and motioning for Kylie to follow. Together they made their way back to the beach and joined the others for a picnic lunch.

Edward was his genial self, engaging with the children the most. They basked in all the attention. Pearl was her usual quiet self, smiling sweetly from time to time, though looking lost in thought. The openness she'd shown up on the rock cliffs was gone.

Kylie was beginning to realize that when her father withdrew and became sullen, his very withdrawing was proof that he had noticed something was wrong but didn't know how to address the problem—or maybe even didn't want to know what the problem was. It seemed he could only maintain his warmth and affection when the surrounding aura was relatively comfortable. A mirroring effect. Maybe that's how she'd been acting too, not only with herself but with Drew as well. Always withdrawing and turning to the violin for comfort and release, for distraction, instead of figuring out what exactly was wrong or lacking. Even prayer was often avoided for this express purpose

—prayer having a tendency to reveal things she felt uncomfortable to face.

But one thing she knew now for certain: the time had come to stop running. Maybe someday her father would stop running too.

Later that day, Mya asked Kylie if Drew could attend church with them in the morning and her kneejerk reaction was to say no—but reflecting back on her conversation with Pearl at the beach, she sent him a simple text message making the request on behalf of his daughter.

He responded almost immediately with a yes and agreed to meet them there.

CHAPTER 17

When they arrived at the church the next morning, Drew was already there, leaning against a tall palm tree waiting. He wore casual pants and a short-sleeved button-down shirt; straightening up when he saw them approaching on the sidewalk.

Kylie yearned to embrace him—felt a sudden pull towards him, an ache in her arms. But she refrained, for though he smiled at her and said hello, the same curious reserve was there as before. Edward gave him a hearty handshake in greeting, Pearl offered a nod. Drew then scooped Keira up into his arms, kissing her curls as she giggled, and followed after Edward and Pearl. Kylie took Mya's hand and they trailed behind.

The girls sat between her and Drew, but though only a few feet from her, he might as well have been in a different row altogether. There was nothing for her to do but to sing the hymns, recite the prayers, listen to the sermon, and wait for the service to be over. She snatched a glimpse of him whenever she could but was careful to avoid detection. Not once did she catch him looking at her. If anything, he was going out of his way not to.

After the service, Edward invited Drew to go golfing with him—to "catch up on old times"—and to Kylie's surprise, Drew agreed. They all said their good-byes and Drew left the church with the plan that Edward would pick him up a little later. Even though she hadn't expected to visit with Drew that afternoon, she felt disappointed anyway. The rest of the afternoon felt gloomy, despite a torrid sun. Pearl retired to her bedroom after lunch and the children wanted to swim. So Kylie went through the motions, thinking about her husband the entire time and wishing he was there with them instead of golfing with Edward: his absence a stronger presence than ever.

This pining for him was nothing new, though it did grow in intensity each month. But his total reserve and formality of late had her decidedly alarmed. What changed? Had he given up and decided to let go? Had he met someone else back in Ontario?

But if he had met someone, why come here only to ignore her? She knew he missed his daughters of course, but did he miss her too?

She considered texting him but as usual didn't know what to say, or where to start. If only she hadn't let Ramiro kiss her! It seemed so silly now—absurd. She'd felt increasingly stupefied leading up to that evening, as though inebriated, but then afterwards, when the fog cleared . . . Deep down she knew part of the temptation had been spite: a desire to get back at Drew for the pornography, to make him feel the same gut-wrenching insecurity and rejection she'd felt.

Now, every time she thought about attempting to communicate with him—to find out if he still wanted to reconcile—the memory of kissing Ramiro Airoso yanked her back like a set of chains around her wrists and ankles, holding her frozen in place.

Monday morning her husband arrived after breakfast to pick up his daughters for a planned outing and Kylie found herself once again hoping he'd invite her to join them. When he didn't, she considered taking the initiative and inviting herself; but he seemed to be in a hurry, almost as if finding it difficult to be in her presence for more than a few minutes at a time.

She hugged the girls good-bye and stood on the portico watching as they walked away down the sun-dappled, tree-lined driveway. When they passed out of sight through the open gates, she went indoors.

Trey had been away again for a few days, likely at Cassidy's house, and Edward had gone to work. Pearl was in the exercize room, Connie busy with housework. Kylie started toward the music room but stopped herself suddenly—remembering her newfound resolve to face her pain rather than drowning it in music. It was going to take time to develop the habit though, probably a long time, with setbacks too. She had to first learn to differentiate between the healthy craving to play the violin as a creative artform versus using it to suppress an inordinate amount of anxiety. Using the violin as a form of avoidance only fed her malaise; increasing the divide between her and Drew.

So she went to her bedroom instead and spent a long time in prayer, pouring out her spirit, laying it all out before God as honestly as she could; seeking his forgiveness for going too far with Ramiro, and asking for guidance and direction with Drew.

Mid-afternoon a knock sounded at the front

door and moments later she heard voices downstairs. Pearl and Ramiro.

And just like that her heart was pounding.

A week had passed since seeing him and she'd begun to hope his hiatus was over; that he'd left the Island on a lengthy cruise ship never to be seen by her again. It would have been so much easier that way.

But no, here he was.

Should she stay put or go downstairs? Instinct told her to hide, to run—but wasn't that the very thing she'd decided to stop doing? No—she needed to go and talk to him, to explain that there was nothing between them and never would be. Closure. How else could she feel at peace with herself again?

Inhaling deeply, she went down the stairs, heart still hammering in her chest, and tried to look casual as though she just happened to be heading that way and didn't know anyone was around.

Ramiro looked up at her, making eye contact with a look of surprise. He smiled. Pearl was still in her pajamas, a box of Band-Aids in her hands. Her countenance fell at the sight of Kylie. Then, with what seemed to be a glare, she pivoted and went straight past her up the stairs, leaving Kylie at the bottom with Ramiro.

"Do you by chance have a couple of minutes

to talk?" she asked him, forcing a friendly smile. Her face was hot; it was difficult to look him in the eyes.

"Certainly." He seemed as casual as ever.

She suggested they step outside, knowing Connie was doing chores around the house and might overhear.

"Sure," he said, "why not walk with me to my bike?"

Nodding assent, she followed him outside, wondering if he could sense how nervous she was.

They walked side by side down the drive-way, a breeze scattering scarlet petals across their path. He made no attempts at conversation, pre-sumably waiting for her to speak first, but her throat felt too tight; she wasn't sure how to begin.

When they reached his scooter she finally broke the silence, awkwardly referencing the past Monday evening when they'd gone to the water-front esplanade together. He gazed down at her with an expression of both reserve and curiosity, probably already knowing what she was going to say. They stood only two feet apart.

Though he looked as gorgeous as she remembered, the mystique was gone somehow. His face was exquisite, but not treasured. She didn't know him. And her heart still belonged to Drew after all—she knew that now.

"I shouldn't have kissed you," she said, stumbling over the word. "I'm married, I should have told you, I'm sorry."

He narrowed an eye almost imperceptibly.

"But you are separated, no?"

"Yes, it's just that—"

"Please, you do not need to explain." A curt smile. "A man can try, can he not? Besides, I enjoyed our duets immensely—thank you." He looked at his wristwatch. "Well my dear, I must be going. I appreciate your concern for me but I am quite fine, and was in no way languishing. Take care of yourself now, it was a pleasure to have met you."

Outside the gates a heavy vehicle could be heard approaching. He reached for his helmet as a pink transit bus slowed to a stop on the other side of the road.

Kylie felt the blood drain from her face as Drew, Mya and Keira stepped down off the bus and crossed the sunny road outside the open gate, closing the gap between them in mere seconds. Drew lifted his sunglasses, setting them atop his head.

Though he wore a courteous expression, she recognized it immediately as a mask, the same look he often wore during social settings with people he didn't know. He nodded a prim greeting at Ramiro and looked to Kylie for an introduction. She mumbled his name and something about him being Pearl's cousin; watching helplessly as the two men shook hands. Ramiro donned his helmet then and mounted the bike, starting the engine. With a wave, he sped off, the air tinged with the scent of gasoline.

The children started up the driveway, seemingly oblivious to the charged atmosphere, and left Kylie and Drew alone together.

Drew slipped his hands into his pockets, struggling to seem nonchalant, pulse racing. Was this just one of many times he was going to have to see Kylie and this—what was the name—Airoso—together?

Already he was traveling ahead to the future when he'd be divorced and sharing custody of the children, Kylie in love with another man, *intimate* with another man . . . He swallowed down a groan and a wave of nausea.

Her face was chalky, Arctic eyes wide with what looked a lot like fear. And no wonder. He'd arrived home with the girls a full hour earlier than she'd expected because it happened to work best with the bus schedule. Had she been meeting up with this man whenever Drew was safely out of the way? The likelihood had already crossed his mind since that first day in the park: of course they would continue to see one another. But he'd held on to a smidgen of hope that somehow it wasn't what he thought, that he'd misread the situation, that there might be a reasonable explanation after all. But now here they were together again; secretly it seemed, since no one else was around . . . not even Pearl, who was supposedly the relative.

"Will you join us for tea today?" she said, catching him off guard. "It's just about that time."

She seemed sincere and he narrowed his eyes, not sure what to make of the invite. In mere seconds, a dozen questions had already raced to his tongue; a dozen accusations too. Where to start though? What to say, what to ask? Whether to be angry or dismayed. And tea time—it's not like they could discuss the situation in front of everyone. Besides, he couldn't sit through tea anyway without losing his composure, not after meeting the specimen face to face. Despondency was already pulling down his features like gravity; he could feel the drag at the corner of his lip, the heaviness in his brow.

Finding this prolonged eye contact too difficult, he removed the sunglasses from his head and slipped them on; then, fidgeting, removed them again and held them loosely in one hand. It killed him to look at her but he managed to mumble a decline, voice tight and breathing shallow.

It wasn't clear if she realized he already knew about Airoso, that he'd seen them together before; it seemed unlikely. But to introduce the man as Pearl's cousin, as though he were nothing more to her . . . She had intended to deceive him. He got it though, having often wondered how long his pornography addiction would have continued, if Kylie hadn't caught him.

She made no response, only stared at him, blinking; eyes wide as though unsure what to say or do next.

Deciding to just make it easy for her, he said good-bye and started toward the road.

"Wait—" she said. "Let me see the kids inside and I'll be right back. Can you spare a few minutes before you go?"

He slowed his step, turned.

Her eyes were pleading now. But pleading what?

Was this it then? Was she going to tell him here and now about the end of their marriage . . . and about that man, Airoso?

Drew nodded and moved to the shade of the nearest tree to wait, watching as she walked up the driveway to the house, summer dress swirling about her ankles.

She returned a couple of minutes later,

approaching him slowly as though unsure of her-self. Nervous probably. He pulled his hands from his pockets but made no other movements. She joined him under the tree and stopped about three feet away, eyes wide and limpid. The air was heavy with the scent of cedar and flowers.

He struggled to hold her gaze, fearing his own eyes would betray him.

She reached out and touched his hand, lift-ing it up in hers, taking a step forward. She looked down and smoothed her thumb over the back of his hand, the warmth of her touch sending a jolt up his arm.

"Drew, I . . . " She searched his face. "I have to tell you."

He wanted to pull his hand away and cross his arms; to brace himself. Instead he stood very still, staring down at her.

"I love you," she said, still searching. "But I've been stumbling around in the fog these past few months—years actually—and I . . . I didn't know how we could possibly move forward, how we could change . . . But the truth is I still love you. Desperately."

His throat tightened, tears filling his eyes. He blinked them back. "Airoso . . . " It was all he could muster.

Her expression changed, clouded. His hand

slipped from hers.

"What do you know?" she asked, brow drawn.

"Only that I saw you with him at Queen Elizabeth park. Completely by chance. Last week. Before you even knew I was on the Island. And he was . . . holding your hands in his." Heat climbed the back of his neck, pulse racing. "I didn't stick around to see more." He felt guilty confessing it, as though he'd deliberately spied on her.

Evident surprise filled her face, and something else. Embarrassment? Shame? A flush mantled her cheeks.

"I'm so sorry, Drew."

No denial. So he was right. And was it worse than he thought? Had they slept together?

He started for the gate. I still love you but it's time to let go, is that what was coming next? He might as well just head straight back to Ontario.

"I only met him a few weeks ago," she said then, "I swear. He's a musician and we . . . Drew — stop, please listen!"

He stopped, turned, heart thrumming in his chest.

She closed the gap between them, hands at her sides. "Let me explain?"

A slight nod, lips taut with anger.

"He made me feel . . . well, not loved, nothing like that . . . but . . . attractive. Desired." The last word was a whisper.

His anger dissipated, shoulders sagging.

"If I hadn't—" He glanced up at the sky. "Then . . . " He shook his head.

"We kissed," she said. "Only once though. That's it, I promise you."

The knowledge was a jab to his heart.

"But you must know, I stopped him because,"—she hugged her arms around her waist—"because I wished he was you. . . . I swear that's the truth."

Drew took a step toward her, relief coursing through his body like an electrical current. He reached out his hand and moved a tendril of curls from her eyes; touched her cheekbone with his fingertips, then cupped her cheek. He moved closer and she held his gaze steady; a hint of shyness in her eyes.

"Baby," he spoke in a reverent tone, their faces only inches apart. "I'm yours if you'll have me. I've never stopped wanting you, not ever! I hurt you badly, I know, but believe me when I say this. No one could ever take your place in my heart. You're Kylie—my Kylie." A tender smile tugged at the corner of his mouth as he gazed down at her.

She lifted his free hand and clutched it in hers, holding it over her heart.

"I want to try again," she said, "start over fresh. Do all the things we wish we'd done the first time. We might let each other down sometimes, but we've got to try . . . we'll go to counselling together —whatever it takes. These last few months apart have been wretched for me. It's not what I want, and I know it's not what you want."

Running footsteps echoed on the driveway, far away.

They looked toward the house.

It was Mya, black hair flapping behind her as she ran. "Mom, Dad," she shouted as she neared them, "come quick! Ms. Connie sent me. Something's wrong with Pearl!"

CHAPTER 18

Kylie and Drew rushed to the house and went up the staircase. Connie waited for them in the open doorway of Pearl's bedroom, one foot in the hallway, the other in the room.

"I've called 911 and Mr. Airoso," she said to Kylie, gesturing for them to enter; her face flushed with obvious fear. "He's on his way back, will be here any minute. Is the gate still open?"

"Yes, yes. What is it—what's happened?" Kylie asked, following the housekeeper into the room, Drew and Mya close behind.

"I think it's an overdose. She's not responding."

Pearl was stretched out on her bed in her pajamas and propped up on the pillows; the coverlet beneath her. Her eyes were closed, skin ashen.

Kylie gasped. "Is she—?"

"No, still alive, but her breathing is quite shallow," Connie explained. "I've tried shouting and shaking her but she won't wake up. She was vomiting half an hour ago, 'tis why I first checked on her. But when I came back a few minutes ago to check again, she was like this—though her eyes were open then. But they had a glassy look about 'em, and she wasn't responding to me. In a trance I think. Her eyes slid shut and it did not seem like falling asleep, so I knew something wasn't right."

On the night table beside the bed stood an open box of Band-Aids.

Connie reached for it, tipping it over her palm. Several bandages fluttered out as she shook it, then a near-empty pill bottle landed in her hand. She held it up for them to see, a pointed look on her face. "These aren't prescription."

And just like that it all made sense. Pearl had secretly been using drugs and hiding the bottles in the Band-Aid box. It must be the same box Kylie found in the guest bedroom dresser when she first arrived; the box that had vanished despite there being several full boxes in the bathrooms.

"What are they?" Kylie asked.

"Opioids of some sort, I gather."

Footsteps pounded up the stairs and Ramiro dashed into the room, shouting at everyone to give him space.

He set down his satchel and bent over Pearl, checking her vital signs. He shook her, called out her name right next to her ear, rubbed his knuckles over her upper lip. After that he sat down on the edge of the bed, pulling a syringe from his bag.

"Wait, what are you doing—" Drew asked, stepping forward.

"You must trust me. It is naloxone." Within seconds Ramiro had given the prepared injection to Pearl's upper arm and returned the syringe to his bag. "Tell the paramedics what I gave her . . . " He snatched a notepad from the night table and scribbled a note on it. "I've written the name here, as they may need to give her more." He tossed the notepad to Connie, not making eye contact with anyone else, and after grabbing his satchel, left the room. His footsteps quickly faded down the stairs.

There was nothing to do but wait. Drew monitored her breathing and within minutes an approaching siren could be heard in the driveway.

"He won't be back," Connie murmured as she passed Kylie near the doorway. "I expect he's made a run for it." Another pointed look. "I think it's rather clear now why he's been coming by so often."

Kylie thought back to the paperback she'd seen Pearl and Ramiro exchange at the park. Edward's guess had been right: the book club Pearl had supposedly been attending for several months was only a ruse. It was most likely how she passed him payment each time too, hidden within the pages. And that scuffing of her finger at Queen Elizabeth Park in front of Kylie and the kids? She must have faked the stumble in order to have a reason to ask Ramiro for a bandage.

"Her breathing is stronger now," Drew said from the bedside, Mya standing wide-eyed next to him.

They all moved out of the way as the paramedics hurried into the room with a stretcher and took over. Then, once the ambulance had gone, the children stayed behind at the house with Connie, who promised to watch them all evening. The next couple of hours passed by in a blur: Kylie phoning her father at work to let him know, the wait for a taxi, the drive to the hospital.

They'd only been in the waiting room half an hour before Edward arrived.

Tie loosened and hanging off one shoulder, his face was flushed, beads of sweat on his brow. He looked stunned. Kylie jumped up from her seat and went to him. "She's okay, Dad, she's going to be okay."

"Oh, thank God." He let out a noisy exhale and crumpled down into a chair, running his hands through his short curls.

She sat next to him and filled him in on everything she knew, which was actually not much; just the bare facts. He asked if she knew why Pearl was addicted to painkillers of all things, but Kylie had no idea. So they waited in somber silence until a nurse eventually came to let them know they could see Pearl now.

"You go first, Dad," she said, standing and gesturing, wanting him to have privacy with his girlfriend. "We'll join you in a little while when you're ready." He nodded and followed after the nurse.

Drew stood behind her and began to rub her shoulders, the warmth in his hands transmitting through her cold body. She sank back against him, tears stinging her eyes. How she'd missed this —him. He wrapped his arms around her and she turned, embracing him—pressing her fingertips into his back as though afraid he'd pull away. She laid her cheek against his chest, inhaling his scent like an elixir; letting him hold her for a long time until their legs grew tired and they finally sat down.

While they waited, holding hands, she tried to process everything that had taken place. A news anchor droned on and on from a flat screen mounted in a corner; various nurses passing through the room on occasion. Drew seemed deep in thought too, his expression grave. He squeezed her hand from time to time. After a while Edward returned to the waiting room to get them.

"She needs sleep," he said, "but she wants to talk to you first, Kylie."

They went into the room and sat in chairs next to Pearl's bed. Her blankets were up to her chest but her arms lay on top, coffee-bean hair framing her face. She looked ten years older without any makeup on; gaunt.

"I am sorry that I lied to you about Ramiro," she said, holding weak eye contact with Kylie, her voice frail. "I was terrified of your father finding out . . . about my addiction." She flicked a glance at Edward who sat closest to her.

"So he isn't your cousin after all?"

"No. He is more than that. He is my baby brother. Yet why would I hide my own brother? It is because I panicked on that first day when you arrived—I was not expecting you so early in the summer, and did not know how to explain." She adjusted the IV infusion in the back of her hand as though it were causing discomfort. "I felt cornered and so I didn't correct him when he said he was my cousin, even though I knew you would disbelieve —and suspect an affair." Another glance at Edward, this one seemingly timid, eyelids fluttering. "I have confessed everything to your father now, and thus am free to tell you everything as well."

"You know by now it was painkillers," she went on with an exhale, "yet I will explain. A couple of years ago when the prescriptions I had for my back injury ran out and I was deemed fully recovered, my doctor would not prescribe any more, of course. Yet what I'd discovered about myself during this period of time was that I felt horrible without them! Absolutely horrible. Something had changed in me. I had migraines and nausea. Depression. I realized they'd been doing much more for me than merely easing the pain of my back.

"Nevertheless, I was able to cope for a few weeks afterwards by exercizing more vigorously than before. It kept me elated in a way,"—she stared up at the ceiling—"and I began to have hope that I would be alright, though I confess that I began to feel increasingly fatigued." She closed her eyes a moment, then focused on Kylie again. "One day I pushed too hard at weight lifting and threw out my back again. It felt like a worse injury than the first. My doctor put me back on the same pills and I can not begin to express the relief that I felt . . . how relaxed I was, how soothed. And the warmth . . . the glorious numbing warmth." A little wave of the hand as though embarrassed.

"I'm sure you can guess the rest. When the new prescription ran out I was desperate, though too afraid to order anything online, or go to the streets. So I decided to contact my brother. Ramiro. I had not seen him in a few years, but I knew he would be there for me and could help me in this regard. It is . . . what he does. This is also why no one knew that I had a brother—I have long been sworn to secrecy about him. It was for his protection."

"But he plays the piano like a professional," Kylie piped up. "Is he not one after all?" No one could fake that.

"Oh yes—yes, he is. He does indeed play on cruise ships throughout the year. That is all very true. The rest of it . . . the rest is done on the side and only for those he trusts, not just for anyone. It is not generosity, however—he makes a 'pretty penny,' as they say. You see he always dreamed of being quite wealthy one day—extraordinarily so— and though he indeed makes a comfortable living as a sophisticated musician, it was not nearly enough . . . he always wanted more and more. I confess I too am accustomed to many luxuries that I could not easily do without."

"The doctor said she might have died without the naloxone injection," Edward cut in, voice heavy with emotion. He reached out and took Pearl's hand; it looked ridiculously small in his.

Pearl gave a slight nod of agreement but didn't look at him, a pink blush appearing on the planes of her cheeks. "Yes, I have given Edward an undue fright. As for my brother, I will not likely see or hear from him again for a very long time, years even," she said. "He will not risk incarceration."

They talked for a few more minutes in hushed tones, Pearl's eyelids becoming more and more droopy. Edward went on to explain that Pearl would be entering a rehab program once it was time to leave the hospital. "But enough about that for tonight," he said finally. "We need to let you sleep, my darling." He stood; Kylie and Drew following suit. They said good-bye and the three of them went out into the corridor.

"I'll be staying here overnight," Edward said, "but you kids go home. I'll keep you posted."

Kylie and Drew went outside, calling a cab, and held hands on the seat between them for the duration of the drive. It was dusk and would soon be dark.

She thought about Trey, her little brother, and felt protective; finding it hard to understand how one sibling could exploit another for money like that, as Ramiro had Pearl. Did he care that his sister might have died? Did he care that she now had to suffer the rigors of withdrawal?

But he'd been so charming, so attractive.

She'd let him kiss her.

After punching in the passcode at the gate, Kylie and Drew walked up the driveway together in the last bit of twilight; wide-spaced lanterns between the poinciana trees lighting the way. The evening air was balmy, sky clear. They reached the top of the driveway and a tiny orange glow hovered in the dark beneath the nearby palmetto. The scent of tobacco wafted toward them. Seconds later Trey stepped out of the shadows and joined them in the dome of light cast by the lights in the portico.

"Hey," he said, intercepting their path, "I just got home a few minutes ago an' Connie filled me in. Pearl okay?"

They discussed the situation for a few minutes before going inside together. At the sound of their arrival, Connie left the kitchen and greeted them in the hallway. "The children are already sound asleep," she said, "and I'm about to serve leftovers. I don't know about Trey but I'm guessing the two of you likely haven't had supper yet?"

Trey excused himself and went upstairs, saying he'd already eaten; and Kylie and Drew gratefully joined Connie in the dining room for a meal. The housekeeper sipped an herbal tea while they ate.

"I honestly didn't know it was drugs," the housekeeper explained, fiddling with the teabag string draped over the side of her mug. "I hope your father will believe me." Worry lines filled her brow. "I knew she was sick though and had my suspicions—I think we all did—but there was never any proof besides vague symptoms. They were very good with the ol' slight of hand, weren't they. I never saw a single pill bottle until this afternoon."

Kylie ate slowly, hungry but not registering the taste of the food. The atmosphere in the room was solemn, each of them contemplative, and when they were done, Connie gathered up her personal belongings and left. Kylie locked the front door behind her and turned to face Drew with a weary half-smile.

She took him by the hand and they held each other's gaze for a while.

"Will you stay?" she asked.

After checking on their children together, they took a few minutes to freshen up, and rejoined each other in Kylie's room.

Moonlight suffused the contours of the furniture, the pastel quilt gray-cast and the pillows extra white. The windows were open and a cedar-scented breeze filtered through the room, along with a hint of saltwater. Tree frogs chirped in the surrounding woodland. Waves rolled up and down the shore. Drew switched on a lamp and pulled her into his arms. She peered up into his sea-green eyes and saw the look of adoration and desire in them, knowing he would see the same in hers.

Their lips met.

Eventually they reclined on the bed, pulling back the blankets, and were soon making love to the melody of distant waves.

Afterwards she lay naked in the crook of his shoulder under the sheets, her hand on his bare chest, toying with the hairs between her fingers; relishing the warmth of his body against hers. Breathing in his cologne, she smiled up at him and he smiled back tenderly; pulling her closer.

When she awoke the next morning he was still there, lying on his side facing her, his short black hair stark against the white of the pillow. He was already awake, stroking the curls framing her face. She met his eyes.

This—this was home.

EPILOGUE

October

Kylie sat down at the family laptop set up on the kitchen table in her Ontario home, and answered the video call from her father.

"How's it going, sweetheart?" He beamed at her, peering into the screen as though he could see better if he looked closer. He was sitting in his library.

She laughed. "You're going to bump your nose if you sit any closer."

They chatted for a while and he filled her in on how Pearl's progress had been since they last spoke. It was going to be a long journey for the two of them but Pearl had her heart set on recovery and Edward was supporting her as best as he could.

"And she's doing rather well all considering,

I'd say. She's got religion now too. It's definitely helping her . . . making a difference. It gives her strength—I can sense it. Don't know if it's for me though, but we shall see." He paused, looking contemplative, and shook his head. "Gosh Kylie, here I thought she didn't love me anymore—meanwhile she thought I didn't love *her*. That's a laugh! And I sure as hell don't care if she gets fat, why would I? Look at me for pity's sake." A chortle. Then his expression sobered.

"Do you know," he went on, "when I thought I'd been made a cuckold, I couldn't bear to think of losing her . . . so I was willing to turn a blind eye to it, much as it pained me. Well, we got that bit wrong, didn't we, Kylie. But I still let things fester. . . . Why did I ever think that was the way to heal a wound?" He tapped his fingertip on the screen, pointing at her. "It's hard to face things, isn't it." He sat back. "So, tell me, how's Drew these days?" He winked.

"Hmm, well, why don't you ask him yourself?" she said with a grin as Drew entered the room and pulled up a chair.

The conversation went on to lighter things for a while, then Edward looked over his shoulder as though he'd heard something. "Your brother's home, I think," he said. "Which reminds me,"—

wide eyes—"did you know that boy can cook? Why just the other night, I come home late from work and find him and the girl—Cassidy—in the kitchen, cooking up a storm. I wouldn't have thought anything of it, but the aroma—" He kissed his fingertips. "I followed my nose all the way to the stove like a lamb to the slaughter. Phenomenal. I was gobsmacked the entire meal—and you should have seen how red-faced he was, hiding a goofy grin the whole time like a shy little school boy. I've never seen him looking so pleased in all his life."

He beamed. "Then, to top it all off, do you know what he tells me? Tells me he started college last month. College! Yes. It's brilliant. The culinary arts, he says. Now wait a minute—you knew that already, didn't you? I can tell by that sly look on your face."

Kylie laughed, heart swelling for her brother.

She caught Drew's eyes then and they shared a happy glance. The light in his eyes danced.

"You think you know a person," her father was saying, shaking his head, looking off to one side. "And when you think you've got them all fig-ured out, you just don't bother to look for anything more. It's like they become, well, blurry, out of focus." He turned back toward the camera with a pensive smile. "I guess all you really know about someone is what they let you see."

A White Rose by Bekah Ferguson

Available on Amazon for Kindle or as Paperback.

Dakota Reilly was fourteen when she lost her virginity.

It wasn't romantic in the slightest. If anything, it was a basic case of statutory rape; but she preferred to tweak the memory here, twist it a little there, until it really did seem exciting and amorous to recall.

Now a successful florist with her own shop, Dakota is used to going from one hunky man to the next. Until she meets Jason Sinclair, a local artist and apparent stoic; a locked door. She is determined to win him, however, and a precarious friendship is forged, despite vast differences in their belief systems. When a gruesome loss shakes her very foundation, she discovers a treasure hidden in the pages of ancient history, and a love she never knew could exist.

★ ★ ★ ★ ★ A Wonderful Story.

Dakota's lifestyle choices made me squirm. To say I was shocked by some of the content would be an understatement, but I could not put this book down. Her transformation from tramp to child of Christ makes a wonderful story. If you can take a few shocks along the way, I know you will love this story too. It is well written and carefully researched. Well done, Bekah. This is a winner. - Gardenergal

★ ★ ★ ★ ★ A Captivating Read!

I love books that I can't put down, and this was another one. I loved following Dakota along on her journey of ups and downs, many of which could have been a part of my life or those of people I know. - Alijoy

★ ★ ★ ★ ★ Loved it!

I had a hard time putting this book down, as the story was always interesting. I wanted more at the end! I will be reading other Bekah Ferguson books for sure! - Amazon Customer

I See You
Finding a strange item locked in a shed, a young woman grows
preoccupied with the cold case disappearance of a child.

The Jaguar
A spotted cub fights starvation when he's banished from his
family of black panthers.